Edison Junior High Library

DATE DUE

PERMA-BOUND®

Cassandra Carter

16 Isn't Always Sweet

Edison Junior High Library

KIMANI
TRU
™

If you purchased this book without a cover you should be aware
that this book is stolen property. It was reported as "unsold and
destroyed" to the publisher, and neither the author nor the
publisher has received any payment for this "stripped book."

16 ISN'T ALWAYS SWEET

ISBN-13: 978-0-373-83097-8
ISBN-10:   0-373-83097-1

© 2008 by Cassandra Carter

All rights reserved. The reproduction, transmission or utilization of this work
in whole or in part in any form by any electronic, mechanical or other means,
now known or hereafter invented, including xerography, photocopying and
recording, or in any information storage or retrieval system, is forbidden
without written permission. For permission please contact Kimani Press,
Editorial Office, 233 Broadway, New York, NY 10279 U.S.A.

This is a work of fiction. Names, characters, places and incidents are
either the product of the author's imagination or are used fictitiously, and
any resemblance to actual persons, living or dead, business establishments,
events or locales is entirely coincidental.

® and TM are trademarks owned and used by the trademark owner and/or
its licensee. Trademarks indicated with ® are registered in the United States
Patent and Trademark Office, the Canadian Trade Marks Office and/or
other countries.

www.KimaniTRU.com

Printed in U.S.A.

Acknowledgment

To He who deserves the most praise. God, thank you for blessing me with this talent and enabling me to learn from my mistakes and go on to accomplish so much. Just as I've been writing since I was a little girl, I pray I can continue to share my vision with the world forever with your guidance.

To all of my fans who have come with me this far, and everybody who has shown me love! To all who have sent their best wishes for my success or put in hard work to help make it so. It means more than I can say. Thank you!

CHAPTER 1

Edison Junior High Library

"Happy Birthday!"

The smoke from all sixteen candles tickled Jordan's nose as she came up from her beautifully decorated birthday cake and into the applause that filled the community center. She couldn't hold back her smile as she took in the cheerful faces around her, and well wishes that swirled around in her head. She was sixteen years old today, and she had been waiting for this moment for as long as she could remember. She was eager to free herself from her parents' rules and take control of her life. This day brought her one step closer to the freedom she craved.

As Jordan's mother took charge and began slicing the cake, hungry guests flocked around the table, giving Jordan a chance to sneak off to the bathroom.

As the door creaked shut behind her, Jordan nearly jumped at the sight of her own reflection. Though her transformation had taken place gradually over the past two weeks, she barely recognized herself. Her gray eyes were no longer shielded by thick lenses. Her metal braces had been removed, and her long black hair had been cut to her shoulders.

Jordan checked herself out in the mirror as she twirled around in the denim Baby Phat dress her parents had finally agreed to buy for her. She had done far too much pleading over the eighty-two-dollar price tag, in her opinion. After all, it was her birthday, and this year she wasn't celebrating just any birthday—this was her *sweet sixteen*. She had just hit a milestone on the journey to womanhood, and everything had to be absolutely perfect. Or at least as close as she could get it.

She frowned as she looked at her petite figure in the mirror. As badly as she wanted to be a woman, she still felt she lacked certain feminine qualities. She glanced at her breasts as if she could somehow will them to grow. She was already well into her junior year of high school, yet she still hadn't graduated from an A-cup.

Jordan pretended to busy herself with the cat logo pendant hanging from her neck where her cleavage should have been, when a harsh cough interrupted her thoughts. She hadn't even noticed the closed stall upon entry.

The occupant of the stall flung the door open, neglecting to flush the toilet. Jordan turned the water on, letting it flow over her freshly manicured hands.

"What are you doing in here? You scared me! I thought I was in here alone," she remarked as she turned off the faucet and shook her hands dry.

Her best friend, Adrienne, didn't bother to respond as she nudged Jordan away from the sink with her elbow. She let the cold water run for a few moments. Her eyes were shut, and it was clear to see she was exhausted by the way her head hung low. Loose strands from Adrienne's updo tickled her cheeks but stuck to her skin only when she splashed a handful of water on her face.

"I should be asking you the same question. This is *your* birthday party. Shouldn't you be out there with everybody else?" she asked, holding her hand over her stomach.

"No kidding. I just came in here to catch my breath for a minute, you know? But you can't expect me to go back out there without you. How long have you been in here?"

"I don't know…I'm sorry."

"Don't be. You just overdid it last night." Jordan was understanding of her friend's hungover condition. She always forgot that her birthday was only one day into the New Year—she anticipated her day more than the holiday.

"What did I miss?"

"Jordan?" Jordan's mother, Olivia, called from the doorway. "Hey, I've been looking all over for you. You don't want any of your cake? I saved you the first piece."

"No, I'm fine."

"Is everything okay in here?" her mother asked, obviously concerned. "Adrienne, are you all right?"

"She's fine. We'll be out in a minute," Jordan was quick to reply, and flashed a phony smile.

"Well, you two better hurry. We're opening presents next!"

Jordan nervously watched as the door shut and her mother disappeared. A sigh escaped her and she turned to assess her friend. "So, how do you feel now? Better?"

"Yeah, I think I'm good." Adrienne tucked a few wild strands into the mass of hair on her head and took a deep breath. She gave herself a quick once-over in the mirror before turning her attention back to Jordan. "So, what'd you wish for, birthday girl?"

"I'm not tellin' or else it won't come true! Now come on. But whatever you do, don't you dare throw up on my dress or these shoes," she joked, pointing at her Baby Phat wedge sandals. She'd had to beg her aunt Lisa for them, and Lisa had put up a tougher fight about the money than her own parents had.

Adrienne rolled her eyes back as she pretended to throw up, causing Jordan to giggle. "That's why your breath stank."

"That's why I hope nobody got you a thing!" Adrienne said as she resumed primping in the mirror.

"You ain't cute. Let's go."

The girls' laughter continued as they rejoined the party. Jordan was glowing as she shuffled through the dancing crowd to where her family was waiting. Her younger brother, Tariq, was only in the first grade, and all they ever did was argue. Now, however, a hug from him upon her arrival lifted her spirits.

Jordan could see the pride in her parents' eyes as they watched her tear at the rainbow of wrapping paper covering presents stacked at least a foot high. Jordan made confetti of the gift wrap as she hummed the song the DJ was spinning in the background.

Half an hour later, she had received several gift cards, two Southpole outfits, body sprays with matching lotions and body washes from Bath & Body Works, and more than a dozen CDs. Now all that was left in her hands was one sizable box. Jordan was beaming. She couldn't wait to see what was in store for her.

CHAPTER 2

strawberry and banana flavors exploded in Jordan's mouth as she and Adrienne leisurely walked the mall with smoothies in hand. It was Friday, and after an especially boring day of school, she was enjoying her free time. All the gift cards she'd gotten for her birthday were already maxed out, and the small amount of money she had with her was burning a hole in her pocket. Her hands were overloaded with bags, yet her eyes continued to scope the mall for spending potential in every store window she passed.

"Hey, guess what?" Adrienne seemed to suddenly perk up. A cherry Jolly Rancher from a twenty-five-cent candy dispenser had kept her quiet until this point.

"What?"

"*Warren* talked to me today." By now, her dimples were unmistakable and her red-stained mouth seemed to sing every word. Any contact with her ex still excited her.

"Adrienne, give it up," Jordan said coldly as she tossed her now-empty plastic cup into a nearby trash can.

"Aw! What kind of friend are you?" Adrienne's jaw dropped in mock surprise.

"I'm just saying you guys have been over now for how many years? Don't you think it's time to move on?"

"Um, that's *months*, bitch. It's been exactly four months and nine days."

"Nice to see you're not counting."

"I can't help it! He's just so...*sexy*." Adrienne seemed to lose herself with thoughts of Warren, and her voice trailed off.

"Please. Do stop there." She's probably envisioning him naked, Jordan thought.

"Jordan! I really think I love him!"

"Adrienne, you went out with the boy for what? A week?"

"Yeah, but we had been talking, you know. We were kickin' it way before then, so do not try and play me. And at least I pull somebody. Damn, what about you?"

The pair slowed as they neared a public sitting area. Jordan was preparing to address her inexperience with boys when someone else suddenly approached.

"Um...excuse me?"

"Can't you see we're talking?" Adrienne snapped at the man who'd interrupted their conversation. He was no more than an inch taller than her, and his deep voice was the only thing that belied his baby face and convinced Jordan he wasn't a teenager.

"Never mind her." Jordan hid her annoyance as she greeted the stranger.

"How are you ladies doing today?"

"All right." Only Jordan answered. Adrienne simply looked at him in disgust as she rotated her candy between her pouty lips.

"That's good to hear. My name is Frankie, and I'm out here reppin' for Dirty Mouf Records." With his introduction, he extended a flyer to Jordan while Adrienne impatiently shifted her weight. She looked ready to gag at his faded T-shirt and jeans resting on his hips. The brown leather belt holding them in place was plain, Jordan noticed, and he wore no jewelry of any kind. His shoes were worn and dirty. The only thing pleasing about him was the occasional whiff of cologne she caught when he moved.

"Shoot. We ain't got all day. What do you want, Frankie?" Adrienne rudely interjected. He was a small-timer in Adrienne's eyes and didn't deserve the time he was wasting. Not to mention, he was probably just some pervert. A woman had to keep her guard up these days.

"Adrienne!" Jordan scolded her friend as she scanned the flimsy piece of paper. The pitch of her voice had risen considerably after reading and re-reading the flyer. She glanced up to see a small cluster of girls nearby and picked up on the commotion surrounding two men.

"What? I'm trying to get in and out of Macy's before they close."

Jordan smacked her lips at the comment. It was only six-thirty.

"Well, if it's of any interest to either of you... Jadian Brown is featured on our artist Yung Fatal's debut single, 'Fast Life,' and production is still looking for a few women to serve as models in the video—"

"I'm there." Frankie didn't even have a chance to finish his sentence before Adrienne answered. Her mood did a complete turnaround at the mere mention of the multiplatinum star.

Jordan would've answered but found herself unable to do so. Her vocal cords were in a knot as she reminded herself to breathe. She vaguely recognized the name of the local label and the advertised musician, but her eyes were glued to a very special eleven letters.

Jadian Brown was all over her walls, from the ceiling to the floor. She was a borderline fanatic. Her family teased her about being obsessed with the rapper, but that didn't bother her. All of her notebooks were covered with her and Jadian's names encirled by scribbled hearts. She had every album he'd ever released. She even knew every last one of his songs by heart.

Only a week after turning sixteen, and she literally had the chance of a lifetime in her hands—to come face-to-face with the man of her dreams.

She felt dizzy picturing her favorite poster, the one taped right above her bed. She'd fantasized for years about his shirtless portrait and had counted all of his tattoos. She almost fainted at the idea of just shaking his hand, let alone looking him in the eye and talking to him.

"Look, the casting call is open, but they're gonna cut off auditions at a certain point. Call the number on the back if you have any questions."

"Thank you." Jordan couldn't muster more than

a whisper. He had no idea how much this meant to her.

The girls were barely able to contain their excitement as they watched Frankie disappear around a corner. They held each other's hands as they jumped for joy and screeched with delight.

"I can't believe this!"

"We're going to meet Jadian Brown! Ahhh!" Jordan screamed. She could feel her hands trembling and her eyes welled with tears of happiness.

"Race you to Macy's!"

The girls took off through the mall, unconcerned with the crowd of customers milling about and nearly tripping over their own feet. Their number-one priority was to find something to wear for the music video tryout, and no one and nothing would stand in their way.

As they held up designer clothes to their frames, all kinds of scenarios and possibilities raced through their minds. Adrienne toyed with the idea of her rising celebrity status at school, while Jordan dreamed of being whisked away by her lyrical prince and living happily ever after.

Jordan was bursting with energy as she took her seat at the dinner table. "You guys will never guess what happened to me today!" she announced to her family, and waited for someone to take the bait. She could feel disappointment creeping up on her as she watched them clear their plates of steak, mashed potatoes and her least favorite vegetable in the world, peas.

"What is it, sweetie?" Her mother's gentle tone finally broke the silence reviving Jordan's glee.

"Jadian Brown is shooting a new video, and I have a chance to be in it!" She sugar-coated the details of the situation in an attempt to ease their skepticism. She wasn't positive it was legit but anything involving Jadian Brown was worth at least checking out.

"Who?" Her father only lifted his head at the mention of the name. He was a burly man. He worked years as an auto mechanic and did a stint in prison decades ago. Jordan was his only daughter and he was ready to take out any boys who even *looked* at her.

"That rapper she likes, honey. The one all over her room." Her mother reassured him with a gentle pat on his hand.

"Oh, him," he grumbled, and then sipped his bottle of beer. He still wore his grease-stained uniform after a long day of work at the auto shop, and his gruff face was smeared with dirt.

"Daddy…" Jordan purred, warming up her daddy's-girl charm to try to get her way.

"No."

"But—"

"Jordan, I've seen the girls in those videos. You're not about to be walking around half-naked and shaking your goods in front of a camera for the world to see. Not now, not ever. I'm not about to sit up here and watch my daughter become some video hoochie. Jordan is too smart for that."

"But, Daddy, I've seen some where the girls were decently dressed," Jordan objected. "What if I—"

"No." Her father was blatantly uncaring and spoke with his mouth full.

"So, when are they going to start filming?" her mother asked. Jordan's smile was now a pitiful sulk. "I don't know. Casting is tomorrow at noon."

"Tomorrow? Oh, sweetie, your little brother has a basketball game tomorrow," her mother said. "See that, you couldn't have gone anyway." Her mother hustled to the kitchen to retrieve the homemade apple pie she'd baked for dessert.

Jordan sighed and propped her head on her hands, her elbows resting on the oak table.

"Get your elbows off the table."

Jordan pouted after being scolded by her father

but didn't utter a word. She looked to her left to see Tariq snickering and narrowed her eyes. He obviously found her misfortune entertaining.

She watched her father for a moment to make sure he hadn't seen the disappointment in her eyes, and began to focus on the staircase beyond. She pictured the sexy outfit she'd purchased earlier and suddenly raised a single eyebrow. Jordan had a plan.

"Hi, Ms. Hayes. Is Adrienne home?" Jordan asked politely as she paced the length of her room.

"Hello? Mom, I got it!" Jordan could hear a few scuffling noises, until a click secured their privacy. "Who's this?"

"Girl, it's me."

"Oh, hey! You'll never guess what I'm doing." As Adrienne spoke, the low beat of "Promise" by Ciara had Jordan hooked.

"What?"

"Practicing my dance moves. I'm about to blow all those byatches out the water tomorrow! Watch! I'm telling you!" she heaved.

"Yeah, um…about that," Jordan said hesitantly.

"That don't sound good. Out with it."

"My parents said I can't go."

"What!"

"I said I can't go."

"No, I heard you loud and clear, but why'd you even ask? What happened?" Adrienne demanded.

"I couldn't help it! They want me to go watch my bratty-ass brother miss every basket he shoots."

"Damn. And I thought *I* was mean." Adrienne chuckled.

"Well, how would you feel? First, my dad starts trippin' about me being a 'video hoochie,' as he called it, and then my mom just happens to throw in that Riq has a game tomorrow. And you know us. We're just one big happy family." Jordan snorted. "Every Saturday we go cheer Tariq on at whatever sport he's participating in *that* season. And while my dad is dying to make him this big-time athlete, I'm missing out on sleeping in on one of the few days of the week I can." She fell back onto her bed and began watching the TV upside down.

"See, that's exactly why I'm happy to be an only child. Plus, I don't even know where my dad is."

"Man! You're going to have to call me tomorrow as soon as you get done and tell me how it went. Do you think you can get some pictures for me? Ooh, or you know what, maybe an autograph?"

"Nope."

"Come on!" Jordan pleaded as she squeezed the

phone between her ear and her shoulder to free her hands.

"Shut up. You're coming with me."

"But I just told you. My parents are *not* having it." She was beginning to break down under the threat of consequences. Something this big was sure to land her in serious trouble.

"And *I'm* telling *you*."

"What if they see it? You know, later, down the line? It's not like I can deny it."

"Then what's done is done. But I doubt that'll happen. How often do your parents really watch BET or MTV?"

"Never." Jordan laughed.

"All right, then. Look, Jordan, for as long as I've known you, you've been crazy about Jadian Brown. I know you're not really going to pass up meeting him, maybe being in a video, all for some stupid basketball game. Would you just stop and listen to what you're saying for a minute? There will always be another Saturday to go watch your brother. This is your turn to make everybody watch *you*."

"If you say so." Jordan sighed.

"And, man, I'm going to have to stop messing with you if you didn't already figure a way to get yourself out of this. I really can't be stressing like this. You're going to fuck around and make me break out," Adrienne said. Jordan pictured her friend examining her face for pimples in the mirror.

"Well…" Jordan shot up in bed, and her eyebrow darted for her hairline once again.

"Atta girl. I knew you had it in you."

"Do you have any idea how long I'm about to be on punishment for this if I get caught?" Jordan asked, though she was really asking herself. She shuddered at the thought of being confined for several weeks inside the very four walls she was looking at now, but she pushed her fears aside. Seeing Jadian would be enough to justify sacrificing her freedom.

"So? Then don't get caught."

Adrienne was right. It was critical that everything go as planned. Still, Jordan realized that she had to be ready for anything.

She tiptoed to her door and poked her head out, scanning the hallway for anyone who might intrude. Tariq especially loved to play private investigator and spy on her. Satisfied with her findings, she retreated and shut her door, pressing the small button by the knob and breaking the "no locked doors" rule of the house. Even with that precaution in effect, she chose to whisper as she outlined her scheme to her partner in crime. "All right, here's the plan."

CHAPTER 3

---

jordan's feet danced on the freezing tile floor of the hallway bathroom as she tried her hardest to block out the horrible taste of the concoction in her mouth. The mixture of Ritz crackers, a can of tuna fish, chicken broth and old pickle juice she'd found in the dark depths of their refrigerator was not at all pleasant, especially at 10:30 a.m., but she knew she would need evidence to back up her claim of food poisoning. She held back the urge to spit as she heard footsteps, and took the steaming hot washcloth from her forehead. The Wright family had been bustling about the house preparing to go to Tariq's basketball game, and someone realized she was missing.

As she let go of the foul mixture, she held her body far from the toilet to amplify the sound effects. Her gagging and choking came naturally.

"What's wrong with you?" She almost wanted to smile when she saw her mother rushing her way. From the worried look on her face, she was already buying her act.

"I think I ate something bad at the mall yesterday."

"Mmm, come here." She pulled her close as she turned her hand to press it against her daughter's forehead. "Yeah, I was wondering why you didn't come down when I called you for breakfast earlier. I just thought you were mad about...well, you know."

"No...I just... Ow...I just want to lay down." She grabbed her stomach as if something were trying to eat its way out, and her face twisted in false pain. "Tell Riq I said good luck?"

She fought to keep from running. She was only three steps from her room when her mother's voice made the hairs on the back of her neck stand on end.

"Who said you're still not going with us?"

"Mom..."

"Jordan Chari Wright, I swear, if you're trying to go to that little video thing or whatever—"

Jordan started choking and threw in a groan for the sake of her performance. She was relieved when her father called from the bottom of the stairway, ordering them to come along before Tariq was late. Her parents didn't have time to interrogate her thoroughly, and she was still in her pajamas. Jordan was proud of her masterful timing for what was playing out right before her eyes.

Her mother didn't say another word to her. She simply shooed Jordan toward her room and burned a stare into her that reminded her just how angry her mother could get. No one wanted to be on the receiving end of a tongue-lashing from Olivia Wright, not even Jordan's father. Her four-foot-ten frame could chase his towering six feet around their house for hours when she had an issue to discuss.

Jordan's breaths came slowly as she held her ear to her bedroom door to listen for the departure of her family. Five minutes had gone by and no one had come knocking at her door. She stuck her head into the hall first, then paused. She heard nothing.

She tiptoed quietly down each step and bent low to pull the curtain back from a living room window. She could feel her impulse for adventure taking over at the sight of the deserted driveway. Their white minivan was nowhere in sight.

Jordan glanced at the clock on the wall and immediately stripped off her pajamas to reveal curve-hugging jeans and a top that was folded to show off her navel. She despised the fact that she couldn't get her belly button pierced until she was eighteen; it was frustrating to see so many of her friends with piercings.

She shook her hair wildly after freeing it from the claws of her hair clip and teased it by grazing her nails against her scalp. She dabbed on a bit of lip gloss, pulled on her stiletto boots and was ready to go by the time Adrienne pulled her Honda up to the curb.

She dashed out of the house and dropped her keys in her excitement as she went to lock the door. She could hear the bass of Jadian's latest project vibrating the coupe, and as she got closer she made out the words. Jordan could barely keep her composure. She was sure her birthday wish was kicking in now, as unbelievable as it was.

In the parking lot of a loft downtown, Adrienne came close to running over the block of cement marking the head of their space. They'd just arrived and they could already hear the chatter coming from the array of women standing in what appeared to be a mile-long line.

"We are never going to get in there before my

parents get home!" Jordan's heart sank, and all hope was gone at the sight of her competition.

"Yes, we will. We have to. We didn't come all this way for nothing. Plus, remember what ol' Frankie boy said, they're going to cut the line at some point, so come on." Adrienne ditched her coat and braved the brisk weather of an Atlanta winter in nothing but closed-toe stilettos, shorts and a strapless lace top with nothing underneath.

"Damn, Adrienne." Jordan put her hands over her eyes after seeing her friend's brazen outfit.

"What? Oh, this?" Adrienne said as she looked herself over. "Girl, I'm trying to get a part for real. Shit, I was watching this show on VH1, and there's money in this. You just gotta get camera time and have people notice you."

"That's all fine and good, but you ain't cold?" Jordan pulled the zipper on her jacket higher. She had mastered the girl-next-door look, but fell short of a seductive vixen.

"Jordan, it's at least a hundred other bitches who done been in there, and even more to go. It's crucial you stand out. You know, leave a lasting impression."

Jordan didn't hesitate to follow Adrienne, who had her game face on. She managed to squeeze them into the line with fake smiles and worthless conversation just in time to catch the eye of a patrolling security guard.

Adrienne casually drew the thirtysomething man into the conversation, and after a lengthy flirtatious exchange he escorted the two girls to the front of the line. Jordan idolized her for getting them indoors in less than an hour.

Jordan's nerves were frayed, and her knees were locked to keep her upright. She and Adrienne had just finished their auditions less than ten minutes apart from each other and now they waited in suspense to hear the outcome. Adrienne had come through on her end with the fake IDs, allowing them to remain while girls their age were turned away. Their palms were clammy, but their grip on each other was solid as they exchanged glances and smiles of encouragement.

Jordan was sure she could feel her body quitting on her as a stone-faced casting director stood and began to call off numbers rapidly, like an auctioneer. She squeezed her eyes shut and prayed she would hear her number.

Jordan listened to the monotonous tone of the casting director and the footsteps of hopefuls who had been eliminated as they collected their things. Tension seemed to replace the oxygen in the room, as one of his assistants held her hand to his ear and whispered something every girl in the room would've loved to hear.

"Ninety-six, one-oh-two, and one-oh-four and one-oh-seven, you may leave and unfortunately that concludes our selection process. But we want to thank you all for coming out and wish you better luck next time."

Jordan's eyebrows came together in the middle of her forehead. She couldn't believe Adrienne had just let go of her hand and was now exiting the room. It pained her to see her friend shove past the remaining finalists and tear her number into pieces. Her angry exit left the occupants of the room in an awkward silence. Jordan watched the paper debris descend from the air to scatter over the scratched hardwood floor like snow.

"Congratulations!" Adrienne was all smiles when she pulled Jordan into a hug and rocked her from side to side in the parking lot. Jordan had expected to have to comfort her, but to her surprise, Adrienne seemed to now be taking her rejection rather well.

"Are you okay?" She made sure to look her friend in the eye for any signs that she was holding back.

"Pshh! Yeah, I was just doing it for fun anyways. Don't nobody really care about that wack-ass video."

"Yeah, same here." Jordan played along to cushion the blow to Adrienne's ego.

"So, what'd they say? When am I going to see you on TV?"

"Shooting is Tuesday, but we're not supposed to tell anybody where."

"Oh, come on. I won't tell anybody." Adrienne playfully stuck her tongue out and bit it while Jordan shot her a look of disbelief.

"Anyway, I'm going to need you to get me all my work from my classes that day so I don't fall behind. I'm going to have to watch my damn mailbox like a hawk with all these unexcused absences I'm racking up."

"You skipped class with me *once* this semester, Jordan."

"I just don't want to get in the habit."

As the Honda's engine roared to life, Jordan clicked her seat belt in place. Adrienne whipped the car out of the parking space, her erratic driving putting Jordan on edge. Adrienne was obviously upset, but she was too proud to show it. She was so stubborn she'd rather have died than admit that someone had hurt her feelings.

Jordan gave her friend space and began biting what was left of her nails to nubs. She was happy, but she had one more hurdle to overcome: making it home before her parents did.

In a desperate effort to relax, she angled her head toward the sky and took a deep breath. She closed her eyes for a moment and smiled inside. Knowing she was one step closer to seeing Jadian was sur-real—but it left her exhilarated. Being sixteen was turning out better than she had ever imagined. All her dreams seemed to be coming true.

CHAPTER 4

"I'm sorry." Jordan apologized to an unfamiliar girl in the school hallway after accidentally stepping on the girl's shoe in her rush. She had to get to Adrienne and fill her in on what had happened after Adrienne had dropped her off on Saturday.

Her parents had lit into her after passing Adrienne on the road, but they hadn't arrived home in time to catch Jordan sneaking back. She had needed all the fifteen minutes it had taken her to change her clothes and cover her tracks. She was in bed when they burst through her door, but they couldn't tell she was shaking with fear under the covers. They had practically trained themselves to see right through her, and usually they did a good job. However, to Jordan's benefit, Tariq's team had won their game, and her parents were elated at the outcome.

"Hey! What happened? Why haven't you called me?" Adrienne leaned against her open locker door as she greeted her friend, who was still fairly far down the hall.

"I'm sorry, but I ended up having to fake being sick all weekend," Jordan told her. "I didn't even touch the phone."

"So what happened? I think they saw me when I was leaving."

"Yeah, they did. I got yelled at and they thought something was up, but I played it off. I seriously thought I was done for."

"And they actually believed you? You're a terrible liar!"

Jordan nodded in agreement, then laughed.

"I'm beginning to think I'm a bad influence on you." Adrienne smirked.

"How can you say that? *You* can't influence *me*, I'm older. It's not supposed to work that way."

"Hey, you're only older than me by a few months! I'm closer to being sixteen than you think. I bet if you ask anybody, they'd think I was older than you." Adrienne spun her combination lock before beginning her trek to class across campus. Jordan followed.

"From January to May is more than a couple months."

"Hey, Jordan, what's up?" Jordan looked up from their chat to see none other than Michelle Jenkins. She and Michelle had been childhood friends, but not even midway into their freshman year of high school Michelle had dropped Jordan because of her looks and shyness. Jordan had been depressed for months after being dissed when all her friends seemed to be accepted. She still remembered what a nightmare something as simple as choosing where to sit at lunch had been.

"Why are you looking at me like that?" Adrienne asked, alarmed at her friend's suspicious expression.

"Because I'm trying to figure out why the hell Michelle just said something to me." Jordan tilted her head to the side, trying to read Adrienne's nervous body language. There was a time when Michelle called the shots and everyone followed, including Jordan. But as soon as Jordan couldn't keep up with the clique, she used her ultra popularity and manipulative ways to dispel her.

"How should I know?"

"Adrienne…"

She let out a sigh. "Farrah and Kenya cornered

me! What was I supposed to do? I have first period with them!"

"Oh, great! Now everybody's going to know!" Jordan cried. It was common knowledge that Kenya Walters, Farrah Harris and Michelle Jenkins were thick as thieves and that none of them could keep a secret to save their lives.

"Why shouldn't they? But don't even trip. I was just chillin' with them first hour 'cause you know I ain't about to change for gym." She laughed, sounding relieved that she'd been found out. "They're actually pretty cool when you get to know 'em."

"No, they're not. They're fake as hell."

"Yeah, because you were the one they turned their backs on once they got to high school. I know the story." Adrienne's words were blunt as she weaved through the bands of hyperactive students in the halls.

"Well, as you so nicely put it, yeah, they did turn on me. And if I were you I'd watch what you say to them. That clique shit may look nice from the outside, but they all got problems."

"I see we got some haters."

"Whatever, say what you want."

"Hell yeah…" Adrienne paused briefly, then continued. "But let me guess, you don't, right?"

"Nope. Not me." Jordan playfully smirked.

"It sure must be nice to be you, then, huh?" She chuckled.

"You could say that."

Adrienne grinned deviously and gently placed her hand on Jordan's shoulder. Her lips moved, but Jordan had to lean into her and listen close to hear her whisper.

"I could, but I wouldn't want to jinx you."

Jordan took a seat at the makeshift dressing table tucked away behind a curtain in the corner of the studio. Her white cotton robe hung loosely over her metallic red bikini as she analyzed her reflection. She held her hair as though it were precious and began to brush it. She was in a daze as she fought to gather her thoughts over the constant murmur of voices and the echo of heels on the floor. This wasn't anything like she imagined, and something told her this wasn't a good idea. However, she felt she'd come too far to walk away.

Setting down her brush, she flipped her hair to the side and leaned forward to oil her legs. She rubbed the slick oil upward, lifting her robe so high that any man's mouth would have watered. She swallowed hard as she peeked around the fabric to a crowd of rambunctious men making catcalls—including the gritty, up-and-coming Yung Fatal.

Jordan jumped at a gentle tap on her shoulder. One of the producers was ushering her along toward the set. Jordan carefully stepped over the many wires that crisscrossed the floor, and she could feel the heat coming from the lights above.

She was in awe as she took her place onstage among a number of other women, all of them intimidatingly beautiful. She felt uneasy under the stares of the crew, and a fierce look from the girl beside her only made things worse.

Once Jadian entered the room, his presence demanded her attention, along with everyone else's. With a single dap, he'd stolen the main rapper's shine effortlessly. She felt foolish for gasping when Jadian appeared, but she couldn't help it. He was unlike anyone she had ever seen, and he was certainly more handsome in person. Everything about him looked perfectly put together and coordinated. The latest jeans hung loosely from his phenomenal physique, and his dazzling jewelry was obviously custom-made. His swagger was graceful. He walked as though the world was his, and he seemed larger than life.

Jordan caught herself staring, and ripped her eyes away from his when he finally shook her hand and greeted her with a friendly hello. She was caught in a whirlwind of emotion, and scolded herself for not speaking. The butterflies in her stomach wouldn't allow her to say a word, and she couldn't think of anything except remembering the exact spot on her hand he'd touched her.

As the director started to shout orders from his chair, Jordan scooted closer to Jadian. She had gotten the same generic reception as all the other girls onstage, but she wanted all of his attention by the end of the day.

As the countdown began, Jordan looked into the distance to calm down. She tried to keep her hands at her sides instead of in front of her exposed stomach, and cringed under the gaze of an unfamiliar man nearby. She unintentionally made eye contact with him, and his grin made her immediately tell herself not to look at him again.

The melody to "Fast Life" flooded the room, and several onlookers bobbed their heads with the rhythm. As Jadian and Yung Fatal stormed the camera, Jordan felt inspired to perform. Her pounding heart was almost too much to bear. It was showtime.

The crew was well into shooting their last set after countless changes in lighting and what felt like endless takes. Jordan nodded off in her chair as she looked on from the sidelines. She wasn't featured in many shots of the video, but she was tired from dancing, and her feet were sore. She'd long since changed back into her everyday clothes, but she couldn't tear herself away from Jadian. He hadn't said anything else to her during the low-budget shoot, but the longer he hung around and mingled, the more it kept her hope alive.

She sat up in her chair, and her applause blended with the hoots and hollers that followed the wrap-up announcement. They checked off their final location and would now edit for the video's premiere.

Jordan didn't falter as the man who had conveyed his interest before filming closed in on her.

"You a big fan of Jay's?" he whispered in her ear from behind, and flashed his diamond-studded grill. For some odd reason, his smooth, raspy voice sent chills down her spine, and her muscles relaxed.

"Maybe."

"Hey, J.B.! J.B.! Wad up?" the mysterious stranger called out to Jadian as a team of assistants surrounded the star.

"Shit, man, I'm just happy it's done. I'm tired as hell, but you know I had to stick around and see my man Fatal do his thing." Jadian ignored the constant nagging of his manager to reply.

Jadian's eyes traveled over to Jordan, but it took her a minute to process reality. She was overwhelmed all over again. The opportunity she'd been craving all day was finally staring her in the face.

"Oh, my bad. Let me introduce you to a friend of mine real quick…" the stranger jumped in, prompting Jordan to speak.

"Jordan. N-nice job today… You were great," she stammered.

"Thanks." Jadian had an emptiness in his eyes that showed he barely remembered her face, but his tone was friendly all the same. Jordan told herself his reaction wasn't anything personal. Things must often have been a blur during his hectic days.

"Jadian! Come on, you were supposed to be at the radio station by eight." The balding manager was now looming over his shoulder and losing his patience.

"What time is it?"

"Eight-thirty." His face was flushed as he pointed at the pricey Bulgari watch on his wrist.

"A'ight then, my nigga. Stay up." Jadian turned his handshake into a pat on the back before being hurried along on business.

"Hmm…that's a nice name. Jordan. I like that."

He was cool and collected as he stuffed his hands deep in his crisp Red Monkey jeans.

"Thank you. I don't think I caught yours?"

"Lorenzo."

"Okay then, Lorenzo, you really didn't have to do that."

"I'm sorry. I thought I was doing you a favor. I saw you go dumb every time someone even said Jadian's name from all the way down here."

"Uh-uh!" She laughed at his joke and took a special liking to his animated eyes and his lively conversation. He was no Jadian, but he was a hundred times more attractive than any boy at school.

"So, Jordan, how old are you?"

"Eighteen." She had been lying about her age from the start, and in makeup, she easily passed as legal.

"Damn, girl, you look twenty," he said with a swift lick of his lips.

"Really? I don't get that a lot."

"Yeah, you got a real pretty face, and your eyes! What color are they?" He bent his knees to be level with her.

"Gray." She batted her eyelashes at the compliment.

"Now, that's some shit for you."

"And how old are you?" she questioned with sass.

"Twenty-one. What you got up for tonight?"

"Uh...nothing... Why?" She was beginning to second-guess her lie. However, her increasing curiosity fueled her deceit.

"What if I told you I might be able to get you some one-on-one time with Jadian later on tonight?"

"Don't play. You can do that?" She was giddy as she grabbed ahold of his forearm.

"Yeah, that's my cousin."

"For real? Get out of here!"

"What I got to lie for?"

"I don't know... He seems so busy." She glanced around the studio at the crew disassembling the equipment.

"Nah, it's cool. Don't even worry about all that. He's having a wrap party at the Grand Hyatt Hotel. I can get you the room number."

"Wait! I don't want him to think I'm a...you know...groupie or nothing."

"Naw, naw, it ain't even like that." Lorenzo chuckled. "He just asked some of his niggas to invite a few females to fall through and keep us company tonight—like on some straight chill-type shit. You didn't even hear that from me though. Keep it on the low."

"What time do you think the party will be over?"

"Probably around two, but there's really no tellin'."

"Two?" Her eyes popped at the hour well past her ten o'clock curfew.

"Is that too late? Am I infringing on your beauty sleep?" he teased.

"Not at all." Jordan put her hand on her hip with attitude. She had made her decision, and there was no changing her mind. She knew her parents would wonder where she was and hoped they wouldn't worry. This was just something she couldn't pass up. She was making the rules for once, and breaking those put in place by her parents gave her such a feeling of empowerment she never wanted to forget it.

"You want to roll with me? I'm about to head over there in a minute." While retrieving his car keys from his pocket, he flaunted a thick stack of hundred-dollar bills to lure her in. He had just pulled more money from his pocket than she'd seen in her lifetime.

"I don't know…" She bit her lip and made sure

not to gawk at his bankroll. She couldn't deny that she was fighting temptation. A taste of the glamorous life she saw on TV couldn't be so bad.

"Come on. You hungry? We can drive through somewhere. I'll get you anything you want."

"Anything?"

"Anything." He draped his arm around her waist, staking his claim as he led her out of the studio and into the darkness of the night.

Jordan sat with her legs crossed on the couch in the elegant hotel suite. Lorenzo had served her a generous drink, and after downing half of her glass in seconds, her face twisted in reaction to the strong alcohol. She knew she had to fit in, so she swallowed the liquor straight, and her lips puckered as she unknowingly sipped sin from her glass: a mixture of gin and Hennessy.

Lorenzo cuddled close to her when he took his seat, but Jordan continued to scan her surroundings for any sign of her favorite musician. It had been more than an hour already and he was still nowhere to be seen.

"I thought you said Jadian was going to be here." She craned her neck to see over the crowd, which was comprised mostly of women.

"Yeah, he will later. I just got a text from him and he said he's getting ready right now," Lorenzo said. "But until then, why don't you talk to me? How'd you like your drink?"

"It was a little strong." She cleared her throat in an attempt to rid it of the tingling sensation the alcohol left behind.

"Was it too much for you to handle?"

"No."

"I was about to say, I don't know what you're going to do. 'Cause if you can't handle that, you definitely can't handle me."

"What?" Jordan looked away from the party and at Lorenzo, who now had his hand on her thigh.

She could feel the pressure for some sort of sexual encounter mounting, and she didn't like it.

"What? Did I say something wrong?" He smiled and squeezed her leg softly, slowly beginning to slide his hand north between her legs. The stretch material made it feel as though his hand had direct contact with her skin. She squirmed in her seat, obviously uncomfortable, and in an instant realized his intentions. He'd used his connection to Jadian—whatever it truly was—to lure her into leaving with him. She would have her chance to vie for his attention, but once the socializing was over, she was to spend the night with him.

Jordan felt as if her back was against the wall, and she began to panic. She was worried she had led him on, and she suddenly wanted to go home. The liquor had dulled her excitement, leaving nothing more than the nagging feeling in the back of her mind that said she was in for one hell of a welcome once she got there.

She had to find a way to escape. "Uh...no, not at all. But you know what, I'd really love another one of these," Jordan said coyly, handing Lorenzo her empty glass.

"Oh, fasho. I'll be right back." Lorenzo stood and kept his eyes on Jordan as long as possible while heading to the bar.

Jordan watched Lorenzo's back as she slithered off the couch and slipped through the door. As soon as she heard the lock click in place, she took off running down the hall to an elevator. She pressed the button and, lucky for her, the doors opened right away. She rushed inside and turned just in time to see the door to the suite open. Sure enough, Lorenzo poked his head out of the room and peered down the hall, causing her to almost break the Close Door button from pushing it so hard and so fast.

Leaning against the wall, Jordan tried to catch her breath, but her stomach dropped when the elevator began its descent. She was going down—and fast.

CHAPTER 5

"**what** the hell has gotten into you?" Jordan's father made the walls rattle with his yelling. His mouth was taut, and the muscles in his face were strained. Several veins bulged from his forehead.

"I don't know." Jordan twiddled her thumbs and kept her eyes lowered to avoid her parents' heated stares. She glanced up only enough to see that it was almost two o'clock in the morning. Her parents had been grilling her for what felt like hours once she'd finally gotten home after a nauseating thirty-minute taxi ride.

As her mother and father took turns chastising her, Jordan zoned out, remembering how she'd had to use two weeks' worth of allowance just to pay the driver. Her buzz was wearing off, her nerves were getting the best of her, and she could feel an intense migraine coming on.

"Well, you better think of something! Where were you?" Jordan felt like curling up into a ball as her father's growls seemed to morph into ferocious roars. His words cut through the stale air and seemed to weigh her down as she struggled to hold herself upright on the uncomfortable dining room chair. She searched his manner for any hint of love or forgiveness. At this point, she would have considered herself lucky to walk away with either.

"You had us worried to death, Jordan!" Her mother's shrill words greatly contrasted with her father's booming voice. "Do you have any idea what time it is? We drove all around town looking for you for hours! We were about to call the cops if you didn't walk through that door in the next hour!" Her mother was livid, her hands clenched at her sides as she circled the table. She looked as though she was going to jump on Jordan at any second.

"I'm sorry." Jordan sniffled as warm tears left streaks down her face.

"You better be sorry! Damn right *you're sorry.*" Her mother was on fire with anger, and Jordan flinched when she invaded her personal space.

"Where were you? And I know that's not alcohol I smell. Jordan, so help me!"

"Mommy! Mommy! Mommy!" Tariq darted into the center of the conflict with a Spider-Man action figure clutched in his tiny hands. He impatiently tugged at his mother's shirt. As their mother bent over to address him, Jordan exhaled a sigh of relief. She was desperate for at least an intermission.

"What are you doing up, Tariq? Go back to bed," David said.

"But I'm hungry," Tariq whined.

"I'll fix you something to eat in a minute, baby. Just let me talk to your sister, okay?"

"But, *Mommy!*"

Olivia shot her husband a look, seeking advice on what to do. He nodded, and to Tariq's delight, his mother kindly led him by hand to the kitchen to prepare him a late-night snack.

Jordan's eyes found her father's as soon as her mother rounded the corner. He didn't even blink, and his arms were folded across his puffed-out chest. She could feel herself shrinking as she swallowed the lump in her throat.

"Go to your room. You're grounded. One month. And don't you think for one minute, Jordan, that we're going to tolerate this kind of behavior now that you're sixteen."

His words came from behind clenched teeth and were barely audible. Nevertheless, Jordan leaped up the flight of stairs. She even skipped more than one step. He didn't have to tell her twice.

Jordan looked over her shoulder as she pressed the receiver to her ear. The ringing tortured her as she crossed her fingers and hoped Adrienne hadn't turned her cell phone off to charge it overnight. She slid deeper under her covers as muffled noises generated static on the line.

"Hello?" Adrienne yawned into the phone.

"Adrienne, wake up," Jordan whispered.

"Jordan?"

"Get up."

"Where are you? Your parents called over here looking for you earlier. They sounded mad as hell!"

"Yeah, I know. I'm home now, though."

"Speak up. I can't hear you."

"I said I'm at home. If I hang up on you out of nowhere, don't be mad at me."

"Okay, but where the hell did you go? Did the shoot really take that long? I thought you were supposed to have been back."

"Ugh, you don't even want to know. I don't even think you'd believe me if I told you."

"Now, *this* sounds worth waking up for in the middle of the night. Hold on, let me grab a Prime."

"Those things are going to kill you, I swear."

"Uh-huh, tell me about it." Jordan could hear her friend inhale the tobacco and pictured her tossing her pack on her nightstand and carelessly dropping her lighter on the carpeted floor, as she usually did.

"I'm grounded for a month. That means no phone, no TV, no MySpace, no nothing."

"*Damn.*"

"It could've been worse."

"A *lot* worse. My mom would've put her foot all up in my ass if I got caught doing some shit like that." She exhaled heavily. "So how'd it go, Ms. Diva?"

"I don't know… I mean, the set was all right, but the guys in his entourage were getting on my nerves, always trying to grab at somebody, and I was there forever. The whole experience is overrated, if you ask me."

"Did you talk to the man, at least?"

"Not really. All he said was hi, and my dumb ass was so googly-eyed I couldn't think of anything to say. For as many times as I rehearsed what I'd say to him if I ever met him, my mind went completely blank."

"Well, what the hell were you doing?"

"He was really busy and I didn't want to interrupt him! I wasn't about to bother him while he was working."

"Yeah right, I would've walked right up to his ass and laid some serious game on him. But at least you got to finally meet him up close."

"Yeah. We even got to do a scene together."

"See! That's my girl! Man, I know you were losing it."

"No, I did good! I held it together."

"As long as you didn't cry or nothing stupid."

Jordan opened her window and peered at the moon shining down on the street below. She watched the wind rustling the few trees lining the sidewalk and enjoyed the sweet scent that settled on the earth after a brief shower.

"So, tell me more," Adrienne urged. "I want to know everything. As a matter of fact, what exactly took so long? Is it supposed to be that hot? Did they use all kinds of special effects or anything?"

"It did take a while, but then I went to this after-party trying to get a chance to really sit and talk with Jadian. Not that that worked, though."

"Damn groupies."

"You're silly." She chuckled. "But naw, it was actually this guy Lorenzo's fault. He was trying to push up on me a little too hard."

"Lorenzo?"

"Yeah. I guess he thought I was going to give him some, but too bad for him. I was sitting there waiting for Jadian to show up, and it just kept getting later and later, so I said forget it and I decided to leave. He was on some sneaky stuff."

"Oh! Now that I think about it, wasn't Jadian on the radio earlier?"

"Yeah, he had to go to the station as soon as we finished," Jordan said, lying down on her bed again.

"Well, I think he said something about leaving for L.A. tonight, but I was only half listening."

"See, I knew Lorenzo was up to something funny! I just wish I would've figured it out sooner so I could've *been* home."

"So, tell me more about this Lorenzo cat. Who was he? A producer or somebody?"

"I don't know. He said some mess about being Jadian's cousin, but I don't really know what he does. I never bothered to ask."

"And you believed him?"

"I know...I know." Jordan sounded ashamed of being so gullible.

"Well, how old was he?" Adrienne asked, sounding outraged at Jordan's lack of information.

"He said he was twenty-one, but who really knows?"

"Twenty-one! Holy shit! Look at you with your fast ass!" She coughed, no doubt having dragged too deeply on her cigar.

Jordan pushed her covers to the foot of her bed and twirled a lock of hair between her fingers. She was staring at the cluster of glow-in-the-dark stars on her ceiling, and before she could respond, a noise had her sitting straight up in bed.

"Sorry, Adrienne, I gotta go. Bye." She hurried to get the words out before returning the cordless telephone to its base on her nightstand.

Jordan turned her back to the door and pulled her sheets high over her shoulders as a sliver of light cut through the shadows. She held her breath at the sight of her father's enormous shadow and pretended to snore lightly as he scanned her bedroom. Cradling a pillow to her chest, she could feel her heart pounding until her father, apparently satisfied that she would cause no more trouble tonight, finally closed the door.

It took Jordan about an hour to settle down. She'd had her eyes clamped shut so tightly when her father had unexpectedly checked on her, that her whole face felt tense and her body rigid. Alone in the darkness, Jordan's eyelids gradually became heavy and fell over her eyes, and she succumbed to sleep.

Midway through her punishment, Jordan found herself eager to begin a day of school. It was the only part of her day that gave her time to socialize, and with the buzz about the video circulating the student body, she didn't mind the attention. She couldn't make it to class without stopping for minute-long interviews or without waving and saying hello to almost each person she passed, regardless of whether she knew them.

Jordan was smiling at everyone on her way to Adrienne's locker when suddenly her smile vanished and she froze. The same people who'd ignored her for the past three years, she realized, now seemed all too happy to see her. Heads turned just to catch a glimpse of her, as though she were a Hollywood celebrity, and gathering observers whispered about her.

Feeling awkward and insecure, Jordan made a

beeline for her destination, but before she reached Adrienne several bystanders moved to block her path.

"Hey, Jordan!" Michelle once again took the initiative to chat with her.

"We saw you in Yung Fatal's new video last night on MTV Jams!" Farrah's eyes sparkled when she talked, and Kenya was quick to throw a question Jordan's way.

"Is it true that you and Jadian hooked up after y'all were done filming?"

Jordan was just about to deny the rumor when she was interrupted. "Hey, where were you? I was waiting for you at my locker." Adrienne surprised Jordan from behind, nodding to greet the others. "Wad up?"

"Hi," the group of girls replied in unison.

"Walk with me to first hour?" Jordan asked Adrienne, her eyes pleading for her rescue.

"See y'all later." Adrienne jerked Jordan away with a tug of her hand and held on to her as she navigated through the crowd. "So, did you see the video yet?"

"No! You know I'm still grounded. No TV for me—how'd it come out?" Jordan could hardly contain her excitement. She couldn't believe she was the only person in school who hadn't seen the video yet, or that it was out so soon.

"I wanted to call you so bad! We gotta go check it out on YouTube or something right now! Skip your first hour?"

"You're crazy! My parents will... I don't even want to think about what they'll do."

"All right, I promise, just this one last time," Adrienne begged, folding her hands as she pleaded to have her way. "Please, please, *please!*"

"Damn you!"

"Ooh, look! There goes Warren's sexy ass." Warren Taylor captured Adrienne's attention as he strutted by with a few of his teammates from the varsity basketball squad. He was so engrossed in conversation, he didn't bother to acknowledge her.

"Why don't you go talk to him?"

"I talked to him all day yesterday," Adrienne snapped. "Why do you think I was so tired when you called? We had just got off the phone not long before that."

"Oh." Jordan didn't know how to take her friend's strange reaction, and it showed in her voice.

A group of young men suddenly cut between the two girls, bumping Adrienne and almost making her lose her balance. She was riled up and raring to go, her fist raised, but one boy in particular had a rugged look that both the girls found tempting. He was bold in his actions, too, and looked Jordan over from head to toe in approval before reluctantly trailing after his friends.

"Damn, did you see that?" Adrienne asked. All traces of irritation were now gone from her voice and were replaced by envy.

"Yeah, who's he?"

"That's Maurice Owens, and he's only the quarterback of the varsity football team. He's a senior—just transferred here from somewhere in Texas. Where have *you* been?"

"*Whoever* he is, he's cute."

"Yeah, you might just want to get on that. You know Sandra Douglas used to go out with him when he first got here, but I think he's single now."

Just as the bell rang, the girls ran for an unoccupied computer lab, sidestepping a permanently grumpy janitor. Jordan was out of breath as she collapsed into a chair and typed the Web address in the browser and expanded the media player to view the video in full-screen format.

"You're going to love it." Adrienne smiled as the introduction came on and the song started to play.

Jordan gasped and put her hands over her mouth as she tried to adjust to seeing herself on film. "Wow! That doesn't even look like me! Do I really look like that? Like, in real life?" She kept the cursor over the rewind button, and after a series of replays, hit Pause. There she was, second from the left of Jadian Brown, multiplatinum rapper and multi-millionaire.

"You done came up! You're hot, girl! And I'm loving that badass bathing suit they had you rockin'."

Adrienne's words were upbeat, but as she leaned over Jordan's shoulder, Jordan could tell she was annoyed and more than a little jealous. Adrienne had always been the pretty one, and now with Jordan getting some attention for a change, their friendship was being tested.

Jordan toyed with silky strands of her hair as she watched the images flashing across the screen, shocked at her own appearance on-screen. She was so used to being invisible. The way she'd been before she managed to tame her frizzy head of hair, get rid of those horribly thick glasses, and successfully correct her overbite and a few crooked teeth.

Now she looked like a life-sized doll, she was in a video, and everyone had no choice but to take notice. Still, Jordan shrugged off what she saw as a delayed reaction. She fully understood that sometimes, it could take a person a while to notice something new, even if it was staring them right in the face.

CHAPTER 6

Jordan sprinted the length of the hallway as she rushed to meet Adrienne in the parking lot for her ride home. She had exhausted the extra test time her teacher had provided after the bell rang. She could feel a headache coming on. Accelerated French was not an easy course, and her teacher was merciless in her grading. Jordan practically jumped at everything she said that involved the word "extra," just to make sure she'd earn more than a passing grade in the class.

Jordan glanced at a clock on the wall as she ran by. Ten minutes hadn't passed after the final bell, and already the school was eerily silent.

She was headed full speed around a corner when she thought she heard footsteps behind her. She turned to look over her shoulder and crashed into what felt like a brick wall.

"Oh! I am so sorry!" Her apology was automatic after she realized she hadn't rammed an object but a person.

Warren smoothed his basketball jersey and his expression turned kind. He and Jordan had been in a few of the same classes over the years, but they'd spoken only a handful of times—nothing but small talk. Still, he and Adrienne having had a short-lived relationship, he and Jordan were familiar with who the other was.

"It's all right. What are you still doing here, anyway?" His skin was a cinnamon shade, and his arms flexed as he held each end of a towel around his shoulders.

"It's not like I want to be!" Jordan protested. "French held me up."

"Oooh! French is definitely not my thing."

"Yeah, you just might want to stick to the court. I've heard you try and pronounce the accents." She laughed at the memory of their days in a French study group the previous year.

"Hey! What are you trying to say?" Warren came up from a nearby water fountain laughing and drying his full lips with his towel. Jordan studied his sleepy brown eyes and the scars on his baby face, which, coupled with his recently grown goatee, made him look like a thug. But his raw appearance didn't fool Jordan, and she smiled at the soft curls that bounced on his head when he walked.

"So, what's new with you?" Jordan asked a bit shyly. "I've heard good things about the team this year."

"Yeah. We're 8–0," Warren answered proudly. "Did you see me in the paper?"

Jordan was impressed, and was glad she wasn't the only one in school enjoying a few minutes of fame. He was someone she could relate to. "I didn't know you were in the paper! When did it run? My dad gets a new one every Sunday and he never throws them away. I'll have to dig and find your article when I get home."

"Just last Sunday. I was cited as the player to watch this year. A couple scouts are already coming to check me out." Warren mimed making a jump shot, breaking into a wide grin as he lowered his arms.

"Uh-oh. Who's coming? Do you know?" She smiled.

"You know what, I'm not even sure yet, but now that I think of it, you should come, too. I'll let you know when I do." He motioned toward the gym, and the pair lollygagged in the corridor to buy more time. Between her vigorous academic schedule and his intensive physical training, neither of them socialized much, so they were both happy for the chance to talk, however briefly.

"I would if I could, but I can't. I'm sorry."

"Yeah, you know, I heard about you being in that 'Fast Life' video. Are you a model? You about to be busy working or something?" Warren stopped at the door to the gym and turned to her. Jordan still had to look up to him even though he only stood a few inches taller than her average five-foot-five height.

"Me? A model?" She had to hold in her laughter. "Oh, no, it's not that. It's just that I'm kind of… grounded right now," she admitted, rolling her eyes.

"What? A nice girl like you, grounded?" Warren laughed. "What'd you do?"

"Basically, I snuck out of the house and got caught," she bragged, refusing to tell him how stressed she'd really been about her little adventure.

"Oooh, you're bad!" A playful shove accompanied his joke. "What's your sentence looking like?"

"I got two weeks to go until a month is up."

"Damn, I see your parents weren't playing. You should be clear, though, I doubt the scouts will be here the first game of the season or anything."

"Yeah. Well, I'll let you get in there," Jordan said

reluctantly, nodding toward the gym. "Your coach is mean as hell." They loitered around the metal double doors that separated them from the school's newly remodeled gym. As they bashfully avoided each other's eyes in the silence, the sounds of yells and sneakers squeaking against the polished court drifted into the hallway.

Warren opened the door a crack and Jordan could see Coach Avery's face turning beet-red. Warren leaned over to peek for himself, doing so just in time to catch his coach hurling a clipboard across the arena and out of bounds. He was in a player's face in seconds, his finger pointing at the boy's nose. His rant was dramatic, and the teen wiped away the specks of saliva that were apparently splattering on his face.

Warren seemed to be immune to the scene. While Jordan watched openmouthed, he smiled and shook his head. Coach Avery's double chin jiggled and his belly bulged far over his slacks. His light brown, seventies-style mustache was comical all by itself.

"He's not half as bad as he seems," Warren told Jordan. "But let me get back in here. You, stay out of trouble." He opened his arms and welcomed her to a hug. His hands came to rest around her waist during their not-so-brief embrace. At that very moment, Adrienne came around the corner, and Jordan could tell she was not at all happy about what she saw.

"Hey, what's going on, y'all?" She had a forced smile on her face to greet them as she sauntered out of the shadows.

Jordan broke her hug with Warren as soon as she saw Adrienne, and her voice quavered when she said, "Hey! We were...uh...just talking about you." She knew how much Adrienne hated to see Warren offer his attention to anyone else. Her friend would see this innocent encounter as a reason to be fiercely jealous.

"And I'm sure you had nothing but nice things to say about me. Isn't that right, Warren?" Adrienne whispered, pressing her double-Ds against his chiseled chest and allowing her hands to roam over his body. She flirtatiously clicked her tongue ring between her teeth in a fearless attempt at calling up what she knew to be one of his sexual fantasies. Jordan had heard about this and many more of Warren's personal preferences from Adrienne, who loved to brag about how his toes curled seconds after she took him in her mouth and how she was sure no other girl would ever come close to giving him the pleasure she did.

"*Bye*, Adrienne."

Warren's face was blank and his words were cold as he joined his teammates at practice. Jordan recalled Adrienne's telling her how he had changed his number and she'd still gotten ahold of it. Why was it that no matter what he did, Adrienne never seemed to get the hint that he was finished with her—or that he'd never intended to be her boyfriend in the first place? Jordan was almost embarrassed for her friend, but she couldn't help feeling guilty about their hug, which she knew Adrienne would see as a betrayal.

She could hear Coach Avery barking at Warren through the door, but the bitter stare Adrienne fixed on her forced her to put her pangs of guilt on the back burner.

"What was that all about?" Adrienne snapped.

"Nothing," Jordan replied, trying to act casual.

"I didn't know you guys were cool like that."

"We're not really, but…"

"But what, then, Jordan?" Adrienne demanded, planting a hand on her hip.

"Damn, chill, Adrienne. We were just talking. We had a couple classes together before, and, hello, we know each other through you, too."

"Yeah, well, what'd he say about me?"

"Nothing."

"How are you going to stand here and lie to my face?"

"Adrienne…"

"Who started talking to who, then?" Adrienne was getting impatient. "And if y'all wasn't talking about me, then what would you have to talk about?"

"Come on, you sound dumb," Jordan answered with a sigh. "Look, I already told you. We really weren't talking about anything."

Her friend folded her arms on her chest and shot her a nasty glare. "Jordan, don't play. I'm not even in the mood."

"Ain't nobody playing with you." Jordan headed for the door. All she wanted was to escape from the tension that was making her feel so awkward.

"So that's what took you so long? I walked all the way back in here looking for your ass and when I get here, I see you all over Warren. How would that look to you? What if you were in my shoes?" She kept up with Jordan's fast pace, marching at her side and continuing to probe her.

"He's not even your boyfriend," Jordan protested, trying to make Adrienne see reason.

"So?"

"You don't really think I like him or something, do you?"

"Oh, I don't know, do you?" Adrienne was gradually losing control of her emotions.

"You should already know the answer to that question, Adrienne, and if you don't, then I don't know what to tell you," Jordan said sadly, shaking her head. "And I was late because I had a test I had to finish up last hour, if you really want to know."

"A test?"

"Yes, a test. I doubt those extra five minutes she gave me even did anything to help my score, though. I don't think I studied hard enough for it."

"Mmm-hmm." Adrienne digested her friend's words skeptically. Her jaw was tight with distrust, and Jordan knew that even though she'd explained the situation, seeds of jealousy had been planted.

"Come on. I'm so ready to be out of here." Jordan stormed out of the building and into the blazing sun. A cool breeze relaxed her, and she gladly inhaled the fresh air. She took a deep breath and listened for Adrienne behind her, but she didn't look back. She kept her eyes focused straight ahead on the lonely car in the lot and waited for another gust of wind to offer relief from the humidity. She was burning up, but she knew Adrienne was on fire in a different sense.

Adrienne stomped after her, and after slamming the driver's-side door and tearing out of the parking lot, she pushed the speed limit on the way home, all the while shooting sideways glances Jordan's way. Jordan could almost hear her analyzing her own appearance and comparing herself to Jordan as though they were rivals. Jordan had on a new pair of pink-and-gray Jordans she'd bought during their last mall outing, and an Akademiks capri set Adrienne had helped her pick out at Man Alive.

Adrienne was wearing heavily creased Air Forces and her terry cloth JLO jumpsuit from more than three seasons ago. As she watched her friend grip the steering wheel tightly with both hands, Jordan knew Adrienne resented her for making her feel inferior.

For the first time in their long friendship, Jordan was shining. She had made drastic improvements in her appearance, and she was known around school for her video appearance. She realized that she posed a threat to the facade Adrienne paraded around school. Adrienne was obviously not at all happy about a social demotion.

A series of commercials transitioned into "Because of You" by Ne-Yo as Adrienne parked the car in the street, but the bouncy feeling of the romantic track didn't affect the friends' moods, and they sat in awkward silence for a moment. Then Jordan got out, slammed the door, slung her bag over her shoulders and skipped up the driveway. As soon as she reached the first stair of the concrete porch, she turned to wave goodbye, but Adrienne was already gone.

Adrienne was smoking her fourth Prime Time as the car skidded around the corner. The screeching of the tires disturbed the peaceful suburban neighborhood and scared tribes of young children at play in their backyards, but she didn't care.

After she inserted a mix into the CD player, the maximum volume of the sound system only added to the problem. She bounced to the beat of Young Buck's "Get Buck" and inhaled the last fumes from her cigar before tossing the butt out the window.

As she watched the needle of the speedometer pass fifty, she refused to ease her foot off the gas pedal. The wind rushed through her window as she merged onto the highway. She recklessly weaved through rush hour traffic on her shortcut home.

Ten minutes and three highway exits later, Adrienne found the stones that served as a path to the front door of the town house apartment she shared with her mother. She was plotting her next move as she tore a leaf from a tree in the complex. The seeds in her stomach had sprouted, and jealousy was taking root.

CHAPTER 7

Jordan submerged her hands in the warm, soapy dishwater as she retrieved another dish. She felt bloated after devouring several hearty bowls of her mother's spicy chili and corn bread, and her body was slowly winding down for bed.

As she tried to analyze Adrienne's sudden change in attitude, a stream of cold water struck her in the leg. Tariq's giggle showed off his missing front teeth, and he mischievously waved the yellow Super Soaker in his hands before scampering off.

"Tariq!" Jordan screamed in annoyance. Her brother seemed to find an infinite number of ways to bother her. "Ugh, he gets on my last nerve!"

"Tariq, what did I tell you about having that toy in the house!" Her mother's slippers smacked the linoleum tiles of the kitchen floor as she yelled at

Tariq in the other room. "Need any help in here?" she asked, handing off another dirty dish to her daughter.

"That's all right. I'm almost done."

"Make sure you wash that big pan out real good."

"*Okay.*"

"Watch your tone," her mother scolded.

"Sorry."

"Hmm, what's wrong with you? You seem like something's the matter. Talk to me." Olivia's acrylic nails grazed her daughter's cheek as she cupped her face with one hand and read her soul through her eyes.

"It's no big deal. I was just thinking. Me and Adrienne got into it earlier."

"Aw, you guys will make up in no time. Don't sweat it."

"I guess."

"Do you mind if I ask you what happened?"

"A boy."

"A boy?" Her mother raised her eyebrows as though she were amazed, but Jordan knew she only did it for the sake of being an active listener.

"Yeah."

"Who?"

"She thinks I like her ex-boyfriend, which is so stupid."

"Oh, I see, I see," Jordan's mother said as she stored a container full of leftovers in the refrigerator. "I'm sure everything will be okay by tomorrow. Why don't you go and get some sleep? I'll take over from here. It's getting late."

"Thank you." Jordan wiped her hands dry on her jeans before sweetly kissing her mother on the cheek. She was grateful to give over her chore. She was tired, and ready for a new day to erase the petty argument with Adrienne from her recollection. Adrienne was a member of her extended family, and she wouldn't trade her for anything or anyone.

Jordan shut her bedroom door and bounced on her mattress after falling on it face-first. Her recently washed sheets were fragrant with fabric softener, and the feel of the cotton on her skin made her eyes close. As she faded into her dreams, she hoped tomorrow would bring her peace and that she wouldn't lose her best friend over something as trivial as a boy.

After waiting for Adrienne at their designated meeting spot, Jordan wandered into the cafeteria alone. She hadn't seen Adrienne all morning, but she stood on the tips of her toes, scanning the crowd for her friend's familiar face. She fought to concentrate, the aroma of food and the constant clatter distracting her. She had skipped breakfast in her morning rush, and her stomach wouldn't stop grumbling.

Adrienne watched from her seat as a confused Jordan searched for her in an ocean of faces. "Ha! Look!" She snickered and tapped Kenya, who was sitting beside her. Michelle and Farrah were quick to take notice and proceeded to mock Jordan as well.

Adrienne had just finished revealing the scandalous, "real" Jordan. She'd told the girls all about what a "backstabber" Jordan was, and how she was after *her* man. She'd said that all Jordan ever did was bad-mouth them when they weren't around. She had let expletives fly from her mouth as she watched them swallow her venomous story whole. She'd even thrown in a few fictional accounts of sexual encounters with various peers to mold their minds. She was going to make Jordan Wright infamous, and if that meant pulling stories from thin air, then so be it.

Seconds after her tirade, Jordan approached her. "Um…Adrienne, can I talk to you real quick?" Her voice was hoarse and her throat was dry. Jordan couldn't make sense of how nervous she felt just asking her friend for a moment of her time.

"Whatever you got to say to me, you can say in front of everybody at this table." Adrienne's smugness made Farrah giggle while in the middle of sipping her juice through a straw. The look on Jordan's face left no doubt as to her vulnerability.

"*Ew!* What's that smell?" With a cartoonish laugh, Michelle moved in for the kill, clamping her nostrils shut with her fingers.

The table then erupted in hysterical laughter, and several people wiped tears from their eyes. Jordan shifted her weight at the insulting remark. She couldn't ignore the negative vibe that seemed to have a chokehold on her neck. It was obvious that she was not welcome at the "popular" table and that, as she feared, the joke had not only been aimed at her, but went over her head.

As Jordan walked away with her head down, she blinked her tears away to shield herself from the trauma of another round of public embarrassment. Crying in front of the entire school was the last thing she needed right now.

The laughter at the lunch table was still alive, but Adrienne leaned back in her chair and silently critiqued Jordan as she rushed to the bathroom. At least, she figured that was where Jordan was heading. For all Adrienne knew, Jordan was already crying her eyes out, and she just had a bad view.

She was picking Jordan apart piece by piece, and she referenced her memory to find material to use against her. For one, if anyone ever cared to ask her, she'd tell them that Jordan had an ugly body and a barely decent face. She debated whether to try something a little more far-fetched and attempt to persuade people that Jordan had been born a boy or something. She knew how much Jordan complained about her small chest, and everyone loved a juicy, shocking rumor. Once someone heard her say it enough, they'd start to believe it.

Jordan was far, far, *far* from a virgin. She'd only tried out for that music video to try to *sleep* with Jadian, but instead she'd made it with some grungy roadie named Lorenzo. At least, that was what Adrienne would tell people. She had enough outrageous claims to last her a lifetime, and a sudden stroke of genius made her decide to preach from her soapbox tomorrow. She was going to make sure Jordan never forgot it. *If she thought today was bad, wait until tomorrow,* she thought. Adrienne's mouth was vicious when she wanted it to be, and she couldn't wait to take in the range of reactions to her comments.

She looked across the cafeteria and her eyes found

Warren, who was watching Jordan exit. What he thought he could do with Jordan, Adrienne had no idea. Not that it mattered. She was confident he would see the light. Sooner or later.

A small voice in her head told her she was cold-hearted, but she blocked it out. *Oh well*, she thought. *All's fair in love and war.*

Jordan's pillow was damp with tears. Her puffy eyes read her alarm clock to see that it was four-thirty. She had been crying all afternoon. She just couldn't understand why Adrienne was treating her this way. Never in her wildest dreams would she have imagined that Adrienne would hurt her. Things had started out so good this year, with her turning sixteen and enjoying the hype about meeting Jadian and the video, but she had a bad feeling things were taking a turn for the worse.

She turned on her stomach and continued to mope, her salty teardrops stinging her face. Her bare walls didn't make her feel any better, yet she didn't regret what she'd done. She'd thought they would, hoping it would be easier to breathe if her room appeared to be more spacious. As soon as she had set foot in the door, she had ripped every single Jadian Brown poster off her wall in a tantrum.

Jordan sat up after hearing the knock on her door. She hastily wiped her face dry and tamed her sniffles before calling, "Come in." Her father appeared in the doorway.

"Here. It's for you." He waved the cordless phone in the air. "What happened in here?" he questioned, looking around in surprise.

"Who is it?" She made sure to turn her head just enough so that he couldn't see her red, glassy eyes. She couldn't withstand a barrage of questions right now. She would never tell a soul about how she had been embarrassed today.

Without answering her question, her father simply handed her the phone. "Make it quick. I was on the other line with your uncle."

"Okay." Jordan held her hand over the mouthpiece and readied herself to speak only when he was out of sight. "Hello?"

"Hey."

"What do you want?" The sound of Adrienne's voice stirred Jordan's anger and her voice was rough. Beneath her hurt, she was furious. She was just still too hurt to do anything but cry.

"I'm sorry about today. That was fucked-up."

"You think?" Her emotions and thoughts were jumbled. Moments earlier, she'd been convinced that their friendship was over, but now the sincerity in Adrienne's voice gave her the impression that they could get to the bottom of their problem, work things out and move on.

Strangely, Jordan felt herself wanting that more than ever, and her urge to cry ceased when Adrienne spoke. She thought it odd that her heart seemed to jump at the chance to talk to her, and she wondered if she could put the ordeal aside with time.

"I'm sorry. It was really stupid and I was acting like such a—"

"A bitch?"

"Yeah."

"But I mean, Adrienne, I don't get it. Why did you do that? What did I do to you? Is it that Warren thing? Because I already told you he's just my friend. I guess that day in the hallway did look a little funny, and I guess if I was in your shoes I'd be mad, too, but I swear I don't even look at him like that. Plus, you just told me you loved him not that long ago. You really think I would do you like that?"

"No... I thought about it, and then after lunch I felt really bad. I was mad and let Michelle and them get all in my ear, and you know how they are. I just sat with them to make you mad and then all that other shit happened..." She sighed. "Man, I am so sorry."

"Oh yeah, I remember. That joke was quite funny to you, from what I saw. What is that even supposed to be about, anyway?"

"It was just a joke, though. You know how it is," Adrienne said lightly. "Everybody be blazin' on everybody. I don't think it's nothing personal. Nobody said they had a problem with you."

"I told you about those girls, though. They're no good, I promise."

"And I see exactly what you mean. All I was thinking was, *Oh shit, Jordan probably thinks I had something to do with what happened.* That's why I had to call you. Will you ever forgive me? Please, don't be mad at me?"

"I don't know…" Jordan took a deep breath. "I guess we're cool then, but, man, I am *not* feeling Michelle and her little friends. Ugh! They're some bitches!"

"You're too much." Adrienne chuckled.

"I'm for real. I should tell all of them about themselves tomorrow."

"Whatever."

"I'm serious."

"Then do it," Adrienne instigated.

"I will."

"I'll believe it when I see it."

"Man, I am so happy we're not fighting anymore." Jordan sighed with relief.

"Yeah, me, too, but I got to go. Warren's on the other line," Adrienne said.

"Oh? In that case, I'll let you go."

"Meet me at my locker tomorrow morning, though? I think we still have a lot of talking we need to do, and I have got to, got to, *got to,* tell you about what Warren said to me last night. I think we're close to getting back together."

"Okay. See you tomorrow."

Adrienne rolled her eyes as she disconnected the line. She tossed the phone across her bedroom and kicked her feet up on her desk.

She smiled. It had been so easy to spin her spider-web of lies, simply because she wanted them to be true. All she needed was time, and her heart told her they would be. As long as Jordan was out the way, of course. Adrienne locked her fingers behind her head and sat back feeling successful. Her mission was accomplished. She shut her eyes and had just started brainstorming a list of damaging rumors to further smear Jordan's reputation when a loud beep from her computer startled her.

She leaned forward in interest and read the alert.

She had a new message on her MySpace account from Thabaddestbitch69 aka Kenya Walters. She read the invitation to join Kenya and her friends for lunch again the next day, and her fingers worked quickly to reply.

As she detailed her message with more lies to be repeated throughout the student population, she betrayed the trust Jordan had in her without a second thought. She spruced up Jordan's empty threats of confrontation and her choice words about the girls.

As the cursor hovered over the send button, Adrienne paused for a moment to grin wickedly. Her eyes were the portals to destruction. She had awakened a part of her personality she had seldom touched until recently, and when she read the words Message sent, she gave herself a mental pat on the back. Adrienne Hayes was going to put Jordan back in her place once and for all.

CHAPTER 8

SOON after sunrise, Jordan routinely braved the mobs of students jamming the halls of her high school in search of Adrienne. She was groggy from a night of poor sleep, but she raced to reach her destination.

She was so immersed in her mission, she was oblivious to the crooked stares from her peers. She also didn't notice Maurice Owens's foot sticking out just enough for her to trip over it. Jordan scrambled to save herself from falling, and shot a stare of anger and confusion back at the congregation of jocks and cheerleaders howling with laughter.

Jordan began to fuss with her hair after finally sighting Adrienne engaged in conversation. The crowd blocking her path parted just enough for her to see Michelle, Kenya and Farrah in her company.

She had been moving with such a determination that once it was gone, she questioned whether it had been there at all. She hesitated to go any farther, but as she stood in the middle of the hall, full of dread, she was shoved into the congestion and soon found herself being pushed in their direction against her will.

"Hey." She gently touched Adrienne's shoulder, and immediately the cackling and chatter between the four girls ended.

"Hi." Adrienne's cheery mood vanished upon Jordan's arrival, and she seemed agitated. She barely even looked at Jordan, and the other girls hushed.

"Humph, speak of the devil," Kenya mumbled. Jordan shifted the weight of her books on her back and tried to dismiss the sassy comment.

"Oh, would you look at that. We were just talking about you," Adrienne said.

"Me?"

"Yeah, me and you, we can't even be cool no more."

"What? Why? I thought—"

"I'm a bitch now, Jordan?" Michelle added, her tone laid-back as she instigated the drama.

"Shit, I wish she would say something disrespectful like that about me," Farrah chimed in, talking about Jordan as if she weren't even there.

"Oh, and that reminds me." Adrienne stepped closer to her, but Jordan didn't move. Adrienne took a deep breath before she set in on her. "I heard you called my girls some bitches, talking real big. But guess what? Bitch, I ain't feelin' *you,* and if you have a problem with them, then you got a problem with me. What? You think you're somebody now because you were in some music video? You think that you can just talk cash shit and ain't nobody going to come step to you and check you on it?"

"Get her!" From somewhere behind her, Jordan picked up an unfamiliar male voice egging on the argument in hopes of a catfight.

"I'm only going to warn you once to watch what you're out here doing, Jordan. Don't think because you shook your ass for five seconds you're just going to come taking shit from me. Because I'll be the one to keep it trill wit chu. I'm not going to be up in your face like these other two-faced bitches be doin' when that video is the only reason anybody up in here knows you fucking exist. You used to be too ugly to expect us all to forget that quick. The only things pretty about you are your eyes." Adrienne's words were projected loudly enough for everyone to hear, and a curious mass was now forming around the girls.

"Fuck you, Adrienne, and you better get out of my face! You is fa real trippin' now!" Adrienne had successfully provoked Jordan, and the anger Jordan had been holding inside gushed forth. She stood rigid with her fists balled at her sides.

"That's why that nigga Maurice said her pussy stank." Adrienne glanced over her shoulder at the crowd and insulted Jordan to no one in particular. Jordan heard laughter all around her, and the longer she stood in the center of the group, the more claustrophobic she felt.

Her eyes darted crazily around the circus, straining to match names with faces and to see who pointed and mocked her. She began to hyperventilate, the first sign of an oncoming panic attack, and she broke through the wall of people to run as fast as she could down the hall.

The door Jordan used as an exit granted Adrienne a glimpse of the overcast weather, then it closed, sending a slight breeze down the corridor. The weak current made her hair flutter, and she felt proudly villainous as she propped one of her hands on her hip.

"Yeah, bitch, you *better* fall back."

* * *

Midnight was approaching, but Jordan was wide-awake. She was weary as she stared at her reflection in the bathroom mirror. The young woman staring back was a mystery she couldn't afford to ignore. She had dissected the layers of her personality and been unable to find any admirable qualities, and now she paid special attention to her outward appearance.

She used to love the dark olive skin tone she'd inherited from her multiracial mother and the plump lips passed down from her African-American father. She used to love her gray eyes, too, but not anymore. Not to mention the fact that she'd been complimented on them so much during her life they weren't that big a deal to her anymore. In fact, she failed to find anything special about herself.

Tears dripped down the sides of her face into the sink. She was sure that if she couldn't see the beauty in herself, then no one else could, either. She would always be just another girl, not worthy of friends or a boyfriend, just another face not worth mentioning. The list went on and on. As her insecurities accumulated, she dug deeper in search of salvation but remained empty-handed.

Knock! Knock! Knock!

"Hey, Jordan, open up! I need to grab my scarf out of there," her mother whispered from the dimly lit hallway.

Jordan dabbed a towel on her face and blew her nose. She wanted to be alone, but she had no choice but to open the door. All she had to do was turn the lock and her mother barged in.

Her nightgown dragged on the floor as she snatched a colorful silk scarf from a cabinet. "Hmm, what are you doing? Thinking about becoming a model or something?" she asked, noticing her daughter's seemingly magnetic relationship with the mirror.

Olivia gently scooted Jordan over to make a place for herself in the mirror as well. She took her time to wrap her hair in the silk scarf. Jordan watched her mom, examining her pretty face. People said the two of them looked alike, but she couldn't see herself in her mother at all.

"So, when are you going to tell me why you've been crying?" Jordan's mom asked as she made a knot in the material and tucked a few stray strands under the edges of the fabric.

"You heard me?"

"I'm your mother. I can practically feel it."

"It's just...I don't think me and Adrienne are

friends anymore, and I doubt we ever will be. She made me look bad in front of everybody. I hate her." Jordan held in the urge to cry and battled a quivering lip. The details of Adrienne's treacherous actions were too painful to recount.

"You know, baby, sometimes that happens. People change and go their separate ways. Maybe it was for the best. You'll see."

"She's been talking about me behind my back."

"Then I say just leave her alone and definitely don't feed into her drama. The story doesn't begin and end with Adrienne, hon. I'm sure you can make some new friends who know how to appreciate you. You just have to make sure you never settle for less than you deserve." Her mother had a firm grip on her shoulders and she looked her in the eyes with all seriousness. "Don't you worry about Adrienne. She'll get what she has coming to her. What goes around comes around."

"But what am I going to do? Sit and wait until karma catches up with her? What if that never happens? You don't even want to hear some of the things she's said about me!" At this point, despite her efforts, Jordan's tears began to flow.

"What she said about you doesn't matter. You just let that go in one ear and out the other. People are always going to talk about you, and not everyone is going to like you, but that's how things are, babe. You're going to have to learn how to not let that kind of thing get to you. If people see that their petty talk bothers you, they'll jump all over the opportunity to hurt you and only make things worse for the both of you."

"Yeah, I guess you're right." Jordan straightened her posture to appear strong, but she was still too weak to find her mother's eyes.

"Now, stop all that crying. Some high school gossip is nothing to cry over. You'll see." She tipped her chin and smirked. Her tone was playful, and Jordan's weeping slowed to a weak, drained laugh.

"Okay."

"You're so beautiful." Her mother stayed for a moment and wiped away a droplet that slipped away from one of the pools still forming at the rims of her daughter's eye. As Jordan watched her mother return to her bedroom, she felt her burdens easing. She wanted to run to her, hug her and thank her, but only did so in her imagination. Her mother had come to her rescue, and all it took was her loving words to make Jordan believe everything was going to be okay.

* * *

A cloud of dust swirled in the air, and Jordan choked violently as it polluted her first steps off the school bus. Adrienne had stopped transporting her to and from school weeks ago, and Jordan was still having a difficult time adapting to her new mode of transportation.

As she began the walk to her house from the inconvenient bus stop blocks away, cruel taunts were thrown like rocks at her back.

"Ugly girl, ugly girl, ugly girl."

A choir of senior girls seated near the rear of the bus never failed to hold their tongues during the ride home, but as soon as Jordan was out of reach, they stuck their heads out the windows and began singing the insult every day.

Jordan had no choice but to endure their cruelty and keep her mouth shut. She was outnumbered, six to one. But today was no ordinary day. It was Valentine's Day, and Jordan was bitter and alone. Other girls worshipped their bouquets of flowers and devoured boxes of rich chocolates, and she felt like an outsider, unloved on a holiday she unwisely took to heart. Her gloomy mood wasn't helped by the overcast weather. While watching others exchange love notes all day, she had been daydreaming about a secret admirer to ease her pain. Seeing Adrienne prance around the halls with a dozen roses didn't make it any easier either, and when the school day was finally over Jordan had welcomed the bumpy ride home. Every hour of the day seemed to torture her in one way or another. She felt like the only girl in the universe without a valentine.

Jordan was unprepared for the eerie silence that met her as she crossed the threshold to her home. She roamed the entire first floor to solve the mystery of where her family was hiding but found no one. No electronics or appliances were in use, and her brother hadn't arrived home from school yet. Jordan was staring out the window for a moment, in a daze as she eyed their minivan, when a thud startled her. It had come from upstairs.

Jordan held on to the banister as she reluctantly climbed the stairs. She was nearly on the second floor when she began to make out the sound of voices in an argument. Jordan crept to the door off her parents' room and pressed her ear against it.

"No, David. That's not the way to go about this. I still think you should let me talk to her." Her mother's words were calm, but Jordan could tell from her tone that her temper was boiling under the surface.

"For what reason? What the fuck is there to talk about? I think we both saw everything we needed to see already. Us and everybody else!" Her father's yell left Jordan paralyzed with fear. She knew all too well what this was about. They'd finally uncovered her dirty little secret, and now they were facing off.

"She had on a bathing suit, David. It's not like the girl was butt-naked. That's no different than going swimming at the pool."

"She might as well have been naked! And I know you're not defending her."

"No."

"Did you have something to do with this shit?"

"No!"

"Olivia?" Her father sounded very suspicious, and Jordan suddenly thought of the talk at dinner that had started it all.

"I said no! I'm just as mad about this as you are!" her mother cried. "She knows she had no business doing what she did! She knows better!"

"What time is it? She should be home any minute."

"It's almost three o'clock."

"In that case, hand me my belt. I don't even want to talk about this anymore."

Jordan's attempt to escape to the sanctity of her

room was interrupted by her father's emergence seconds later, and she shook at the sight of the leather belt in his hands. She didn't feel safe being near him and took notice of the veins bulging in his arms. She imagined the strength those arms were capable of exerting, and she pressed her back hard against the wall in a state of panic.

The fury in his eyes made Jordan feel like she was shrinking. She began to whimper after he took his first step toward her, his eyes glazed.

"David…" Jordan's mother came after him and put a hand on his arm to stop him.

His hands curled around the leather, and her mother exercised patience as he struggled to snatch his arm away from her. His face was grim, and she squeezed tightly until he broke away from her hold.

Jordan slid down the smooth surface of the wall to the carpeted floor, where she began to sob. Her father dropped the belt and stomped down the staircase and out the front door.

Once he was out of sight, her mother's worried look turned into a scowl. She looked down at her daughter and snatched her off the floor by the collar of her shirt.

"What the fuck were you thinking?" she shouted as she shoved Jordan into her bedroom and onto her bed.

Edison Junior High Library

"I don't know…" Her head bowed, Jordan's mind was reeling with regret, and her tears showed no signs of slowing. She had gotten herself into what seemed like a never-ending mess.

"You never do, Jordan. That's the thing. But then again, this is my fault, too. I knew your ass was up to something that day. I should've just made you come with us and then none of this would've ever happened!" She marched back and forth in a fit. "And then you had the *audacity* to look me in the eye and lie to me? I'm up here trying to help you, and the whole time you're up here playin' me! I trusted you, Jordan!" Her finger was in Jordan's face and her long fingernails almost poked Jordan in the eye, causing her to flinch. She had been expecting a severe whopping, and her mother's angry gestures made her even more frightened.

Jordan opened her mouth to begin the lengthy apology forming in her mind, but her mother wasn't through. "I will not be made a fool of, Jordan. You need to learn how to think about somebody else before you just go out and do something, especially something like that at your age. What do you expect your father to say if someone asks about it at work because they saw the video, huh? How does that look, him having to admit that his sixteen-year-old daughter disobeyed him for some no-talent pretty-boy rapper? I know I'm not going to let anyone think we gave you permission to do it. You think this looks good for us as your parents?"

Jordan only managed to shake her head in reply.

"Didn't think so. I watched that video and repeatedly asked myself, *What the hell was Jordan thinking?* You're lucky your father didn't just beat the hell out of you, and you better pray your grandparents don't somehow hear about this!"

Her mother then paused for a moment and placed her hand on her forehead. She had been screaming very loudly. She shut her eyes, took a deep breath and indulged in a brief period of silence before continuing. "Look, I need to go talk to your father. I'm sure we're not going out to dinner anymore. Thanks for ruining *my* Valentine's Day."

"Are you *that* mad at me?" Jordan asked through gasps. She turned her back on her mother and sought refuge in the bleak view from her window. She labored to accept the reality that the damage she had caused her relationship with her mother was possibly irreparable.

"I'm not mad, Jordan. I'm just disappointed."

As soon as the door clicked shut, Jordan buried her head in her pillow and began to bawl. She knew exactly how her mother felt.

CHAPTER 9

BAGS were beginning to form under Jordan's eyes after repeated nights of restlessness. She had been lying awake for hours at night wondering how she and Adrienne had gone from best friends to enemies in a matter of days. Already Adrienne seemed to have not only one but a group of new "best" friends—she, Michelle, Kenya and Farrah were always together. She had apparently put her friendship with Jordan behind her as if it had meant nothing to her.

Jordan had seen the evidence herself on Adrienne's MySpace page: she had cut Jordan out of all her pictures and started replacing the memories they'd shared with new ones. She and her new friends were in love with their digital cameras, and they'd been brightening the hallways at school with their paparazzi-like photo sessions. They couldn't get enough of themselves. To ease her pain, Jordan had deleted her own MySpace account so she wouldn't be tempted to dwell on the past.

At school one morning, Jordan laid her head down on her desk and folded her hands under her chin. She was long overdue for a good night's sleep, and she couldn't wait to catch up on her rest. It had been weeks since she'd been caught sneaking behind her parents' backs, and she had done as her mother had said by making sure to distance herself from Adrienne.

Meanwhile, the classroom was abuzz with conversation and jokes, and several young men were roughhousing at the other end of the room. The substitute relaxed at the teacher's desk and enjoyed a graphic sci-fi novel in the middle of the chaos. Just as Jordan closed her eyes, someone sat in the unoccupied desk in front of her.

"Hey, Jordan." Jordan put forth only enough effort to peek with one eye to identify exactly who'd requested a conversation with her. Her muscles relaxed when she recognized the familiar face of Eva Parker. The two were cordial acquaintances, despite Eva's lowerclassman rank as a sophomore, and had attended the same middle school.

"Wad up?" Jordan yawned and rubbed her eyes.

"Nothing... Bored..."

"Oh."

"So! What's new with you?" A cheerleader, Eva always seemed to be bursting with energy.

"Not much. You?"

"Same. Well, except that and me and Demetrius go out now."

"Demetrius?"

"Oh, you might not know him. He graduated from here like two years ago."

"Oh yeah, I think I remember who you're talking about now," Jordan lied through her yawn, and laid her head back on her desk, her binder serving as the best pillow available.

"Jordan?"

"Yeah, Eva?"

"Can I ask you something?" Eva asked, her voice lowering.

"Go ahead," Jordan mumbled.

"Well, it's just that me and Demetrius have been talking for a while, and we just started officially going out not that long ago. Our one-month anniversary is this Saturday, and I want to do something really, really special for him. Something he'll remember."

"What were you thinking about doing? Do you have any ideas yet?"

"That's where you come in," Eva said, her eyes sparkling.

"Sure, I can help you think of something to do."

"No, that's not it." Eva chuckled. "You see, I know it's kind of personal, and I don't want you to get mad at me or anything, but I need your...shall I say, *expertise* on a certain matter."

"And what would that be?" Jordan became defensive. She could sense where this was heading.

"Well...didn't you used to mess with that one guy from Jadian's crew?"

"No..." Jordan's voice was dull as she gave her answer. Adrienne had already made sure every last student in school knew about her going to the hotel with Lorenzo. There were more versions of the event being circulated than Jordan could count.

"And he was older, right?"

Jordan simply shrugged her shoulders for a reply.

"Was he in the video?"

"Look, I don't see how this has anything to do—"

"Oh, girl, I'm sorry."

Eva tried to laugh off her question as though it meant nothing, but Jordan knew she was looking for at least a little information about the music video. She just never had the opportunity until now. It was like no one would be caught dead talking to Jordan where everyone could see them. It was as though they thought her bad reputation was contagious. Jordan sighed inwardly, remembering what people said about it always being the quiet ones who were the wildest. She knew her silence about the video made all the rumors that much more believable.

"It's just, don't you think older guys expect a little more?" Eva prodded. "He's in college and he could be with a grown woman if he wanted to, and she could do whatever she wanted whenever she wanted. Let's just say I want to get rid of any doubts he may have about our relationship or me. I'm just not really sure how to go about it, you know? I don't want him to think I'm bad at it, but I only tried it once for like two seconds and I couldn't do it and—" Eva rambled on in her irritating, childlike voice.

"Whoa, whoa, hold up. Say what now?" Jordan interrupted, shocked at what she was hearing.

"What's your technique? How do you do it? I've heard all kinds of different stuff, but I want someone who really knows what they're doing to tell me."

"Technique? Technique for…?"

"You know." Eva leaned closer over the desk and whispered in her ear. "Giving head."

"Oh, hell naw!" Jordan lost control of her temper and shot up from her chair. She cocked her head to the side and looked Eva over with a doubt in her eyes that questioned the girl's sanity. Jordan knew all about the rumors making the rounds, but aside from Adrienne, no one had confronted her about them.

"Shh! It's okay!" Eva whispered. "It's not like I look at you like you're nasty or anything. Just sit back down."

The substitute's calls met Jordan's back as she stormed out of class, not even halfway into the first hour of the day. The door to the bathroom smacked the wall, and the echo was deafening as Jordan barricaded herself in a stall in an attempt to calm herself.

She was out of breath as she squinted to read the graffiti on the wall. "Jordan is a ho" was written in black marker on the wall. Jordan frantically licked two of her fingers and tried to rub the ink away, but even her best efforts didn't manage to fade or smear the color, let alone erase it.

Just as the ink refused to disappear, it seemed her

problems with Adrienne wouldn't go away. She had kept her distance in hopes of falling off her ex-best friend's radar, but even though it had been weeks since their last face-to-face interaction, Adrienne clearly hadn't stopped talking about her to anyone who would listen. Her peers were still judging her, labeling her and shunning her because of Adrienne's lies.

It had gone on long enough. Storming down the hall, Jordan burst into the musty ladies' locker room in search of Adrienne. The room was quiet except for the sound of dripping water from sink and shower faucets, but Jordan still searched row after row of lockers. She sniffed the air after picking up the scent of tobacco and followed her instincts to a drawn curtain in the showers.

She crept over the damp floor and quickly snatched the curtain open. Adrienne twitched at the sudden disturbance and was temporarily stiff with fear until she realized she hadn't been caught by a member of the faculty. She nonchalantly crushed her cigar with her heel, blowing smoke in Jordan's face.

"Move!" Adrienne's tone was menacing.

"Fuck you!" Jordan's tolerance was gone, her anger consumed her. Adrienne had robbed her of so much happiness this year, she felt it was urgent to confront her. The disrespect had to end.

"Ha, Jordan's mad. You mad, Jordan?" Even if Adrienne was afraid of the fire in Jordan's eyes, Jordan knew she wouldn't back down. And she didn't care if her challenging words fueled Jordan's temper. "Yeah, you mad."

Jordan used both hands to push Adrienne against the wall. She wanted to punch her in the face, but she boasted a steady straight-A academic performance and she had a clean record. She'd made it all the way to her junior year of high school without getting into a fight, and she didn't want to destroy what she had worked so hard to build. Her mother's voice rang in her ears and convinced her to keep her fists at her side.

"What are you going to do, hit me?" Adrienne laughed weakly before shoving Jordan's shoulder with her own and taking a seat on a bench.

"What the fuck is up with you telling all these people I go down? Eva Parker just sat up here and asked me for my 'technique.'"

"Who said I told Eva that? Did *she* tell you I said that?"

"No, but it's not like she needs to. I know you did it, Adrienne."

"Whatever, Jordan. Just because your business is out in the streets, don't be mad at me. It ain't my fault," Adrienne said with a shrug.

"You can't be serious."

"Oh, but I am. Do I look like I'm playin' games with you?" Adrienne asked spitefully, pushing Jordan even closer to the edge. "Are you done now?"

"Far from it. The next time I see you outside school—"

"*Oooh*, sounds exciting! Really," Adrienne said sarcastically. "I'm sorry for having to cut our lovely little chat short, but I have somewhere I need to be."

"And to think you used to be my best friend—or at least you were supposed to be my best friend." Jordan spoke aloud as though she were no longer talking to Adrienne, but Adrienne couldn't resist saying something in return.

"Boo-hoo, cry me a fucking river. You're right, I'm not your friend anymore, get over it."

"Well, with all that being said and done, I wish you the best. I really do," Jordan told her. "And I really hope your *fat ass* is on your way to class for once! You could stand to drop a few pounds there, *buddy*." She matched Adrienne's sarcasm, looking her over from head to toe. Adrienne had always been sensitive about her weight, even though she was constantly complimented on her "thick" figure by men of all ages.

"Oh, so you're a comedienne now? Don't get me started on you."

"Actually, I think you've done more than enough to prove you're the *funny* person here. What happened to you? Why couldn't you just come and talk to me?"

"Jordan?" Adrienne's voice was without emotion as she reached into her locker to retrieve a tiny bottle of Calgon body mist. She sprayed the air around her with the perfume and stepped into the vapors.

"Adrienne," Jordan grumbled, twisting her neck with attitude.

"Do me one last favor, just for me? If you do this, you have my word I'll leave you alone," Adrienne crooned as she slammed her locker shut. Her speech was plain and her eyes were cold, but she placed her hands on Jordan's shoulders to force eye contact.

"What do you want from me?" Jordan's puzzlement was apparent as she held their stare. Adrienne knew she had her right where she wanted her.

"Jordan…" She sighed deeply. "Kill your fucking self." And with that harsh statement, Adrienne let go and made her exit, leaving Jordan at a loss for words.

* * *

Jordan sat with her knees to her chest in bathwater that was no longer warm. She laid her head on her knees and continued to weep. She lifted her head in search of the disposable razor she'd placed nearby, and her pruny fingertips felt blindly in the room illuminated only by a ray of moonlight coming through the small window. Her fingers were careful as they handled the sharp blade, and she fought to keep her crying quiet. She didn't want to wake anyone.

She replayed the locker room scene between her and Adrienne over and over again in her mind. Adrienne had made her cruel request as though it were reasonable, a genuine favor eligible for consideration. Jordan had been humiliated in front of the entire school, and now she walked the halls every day alone. She even went without lunch just to bypass the embarrassment of dining without company. She'd withdrawn from the social scene.

She was frustrated with her life, and she bit down on her lip, tossing the plastic blade into the darkness. Who does Adrienne think she is? she thought, her sadness mixing with anger. She barely heard it ricochet off the corner of the room over her heavy sobs. She hugged her legs tighter and began to shiver in the cooling water. Lost in a daze, she'd been drowning in depression, and she didn't want someone else to save her, as much as she wanted to save herself.

CHAPTER 10

"**Jordan** Wright?"

"Here."

Jordan lowered her hand and shifted in her chair as her computer technology teacher, Mr. Reaves, finally reached the end of the attendance list. The fact that she had made it to the last period of the day was nothing short of a huge disappointment. She just wanted school to be over with. After reaching rock bottom last night, she didn't want to go to school at all, but her parents wouldn't listen to another request to remain at home. She'd had no choice.

As Mr. Reaves began outlining the day's lesson, an earsplitting alarm began to sound and a flash of white light came from the strobe on the wall. Jordan sighed in displeasure as she stood, pushed her chair under her desk and joined the horde packed into the hallway. The fire drill had everyone headed for an exit, and the students were more than happy to miss part of the hour.

While others carried on conversations and made plans for the weekend, Jordan quietly flowed with the crowd. She was in no rush to head into the heat that awaited her outside. As she approached the door, her blank expression turned into an angry stare. The glitter on a banner for the Spring Fling had caught her eye, and she wished no one were around so she could rip it to shreds. The Spring Fling was the biggest end-of-the-year party besides the prom, and it had a reputation as always being a hype and memorable night.

"Hey, Jordan! Wait up!"

Jordan became irritated as soon as she heard someone behind her calling her name. She was sure this was just another one of Adrienne's tricks or someone coming to ask about one of the lies everyone had heard about her. She looked back and, pleasantly surprised, allowed other students to pass her as she waited to greet a glowing Warren Taylor.

"What up doe, Jordan? Where you been at? I swear, I never see you around anymore."

Jordan was equally happy to see him and was

about to reply when she hesitated. She could sense someone staring at her, and when she looked to her left, she saw that Adrienne was no more than ten feet away.

Adrienne shifted her weight in her high heels and tapped her friends to point out Warren and Jordan's interaction. Jordan immediately turned to leave in a hurry, but Warren was quick to take hold of her wrist and gently pull her back to him.

"Where are you going?" he asked, almost yelling to be heard over the alarm.

Jordan refused to answer him in words. Instead, she looked beyond him to the four girls watching her. Warren glanced over his shoulder and glared at Adrienne and her crew. They instantly began to play innocent, pretending to be in the middle of an intense conversation. Warren flashed the girls a sour face that let them know he saw right through their act.

"Don't worry about them. Let's go." He draped his arm over Jordan's shoulders and led her through the double doors. Casting a last backward glance, Jordan was almost pleased to see the angry look on Adrienne's face.

Adrienne was infuriated seeing Warren devote his attention to Jordan. She'd already watched him be late for practice just to talk to Jordan, something he'd never done for anyone. She could feel hurt brewing beneath her jealousy as she realized that it wasn't Jordan who was interested in Warren, but vice versa.

"I wouldn't have that shit if I was you." Kenya was the first to offer her opinion, and Michelle didn't waste any time offering her two cents, either.

"Hell yeah, who does she think she is, all up in your face with him? It looks like she's just trying to start some shit to me."

"I know, right? Adrienne, girl, what are you going to do?" Farrah asked. All eyes were on Adrienne, and she knew the girls were hoping to see a fight between the ex-best friends. She stared off into space.

"Shh! Be quiet. Don't worry, I got this," she snapped.

"It don't look like it to me," Michelle remarked.

"Yeah, well, sometimes looks can be deceiving." Without warning, Adrienne stormed off full of attitude, and a teacher was soon behind the trio, ushering them out of the building.

Meanwhile, once outside, Jordan quickly removed Warren's arm from her shoulders. "Leave me alone." Jordan's mood was foul, and it seeped into her speech as she shook free from under his arm.

"What?"

"You heard me!"

"Aw, are we having a bad day?" Warren asked, turning his mouth down in an exaggerated pout.

"You have no idea."

"Then why don't you tell me all about it?" Warren was genuine as he stood his ground.

"It's nothing. I'm all right." As mad as she was, Jordan still didn't want to bad-mouth Adrienne. "I'm sorry…" She sighed. "What about you? How have you been?"

"Great. I just found out North Carolina is going to come to scout me at our next game," Warren said proudly.

"Wow! Congratulations!" Jordan's eyes lit up.

"Yeah, I'm excited. We play the Hornets," he said, waving a hand dismissively, "and everybody and they momma knows I'm about to show out."

Jordan was amused at Warren's arrogance. "You think you're just going to stunt on 'em that easy, eh?" she teased, folding her arms over her chest.

"That's right," Warren asserted.

"Yeah, my little brother just joined the rec-and-ed team last month so he can keep playing all year," Jordan told him.

"That's what it is. That's one smart brother you got there." He supported his choice with a certain overbearing pride in his voice. Warren wasn't just pursuing the sport for financial gain; he had true love for the game.

"How long have you been playing ball?"

"Damn…probably since I was about five or six."

"Ha, that's funny."

"What?"

"Nothing, it's just that he's the same age now as you were when you started," she said.

"Yeah, hopefully I'll make it to the NBA one day… Speaking of making it, have you starred in any more videos, Ms. Soon-To-Be-Famous?" he joked lightly.

"Uh-uh, and I really don't want to. Trust me." She giggled. "The only thing I've been doing lately is getting a head start on college apps so when the fall comes I won't have to stress about it."

"I should do that, too."

"You don't even have that problem, though. You're not even in your senior year yet and you already got college scouts checkin' you out. That says a lot."

"Yeah, but I want to keep my options open."

"Where are you trying to go? If I were you I would get as far away from here as possible."

"It's funny you say that, because I was actually looking to go somewhere up north. Where, though, is the question. I won't go anywhere that doesn't have a team."

"Have you already figured out what you want to major in? That is, if you're not playing ball in the NBA by then. I know I sure can't make up my mind."

"I was thinking…medicine. I've always wanted to be a doctor like my granddad."

"A doctor?" Jordan couldn't catch her chuckle before it escaped her throat.

"Yeah, what's wrong with that?" Warren raised an eyebrow.

"Nothing, it's just I guess it's not true then when they say that all jocks are dumb."

"Hey, I resent that!" He laughed. "Naw, but for real, you want to know something? It's ridiculous how much I read. People would think I was such a nerd if they really knew."

"That's probably just because they're so used to seeing you in a different light. You're Mr. All-Star. Not some Einstein. No offense."

"None taken."

"Well, if it helps, *I* don't think you're a nerd."

Warren cracked a smile, and Jordan felt foolish for her comment. A wave of relief washed over her when the bell sounded for everyone to return to their classrooms.

"So…what do you got up for the weekend?" As the two started toward the building, Warren kept their conversation alive.

"Absolutely nothing."

"Nothing at all? That I find hard to believe. I know you probably be out every weekend. Niggas are probably damn near knockin' your door down."

"That's not even true."

"And I know you probably go out and party with your girlfriends. You and Adrienne used to be tight, right?"

"Yeah, but I wonder how I did it sometimes. How do you deal with her?"

"I don't. Shit, you do not have to tell me she got a fucked-up attitude. Trust."

"But she always made it seem like y'all were kickin' it and whatnot. Plus, I saw her with a bunch of flowers on V Day. I just assumed you bought them for her."

"What?" His eyes were wide and his laughter was loud. "Are you for real?"

"As serious as a heart attack," she said.

"Man, Adrienne is a jump! Who *knows* what fool bought her those flowers. But I won't lie to you, I know you know I used to mess with her at the beginning of the year. I only ended up going out with her because she wouldn't leave me alone! And I should've known better than to give in, because sure enough, she got way too clingy, way too fast. If it makes you feel any better, it really doesn't go any deeper than that," he admitted. "And besides, like I was telling you before, don't sweat her bullshit. Adrienne is all talk. All she does is run her mouth, and anybody who knows better knows talk is cheap. It will all blow over in time. You just don't let her come in between us. We're still friends, regardless of whatever she says."

"Ha, in that case, you're more like my *only* friend." Jordan had to laugh at the sad reality.

"Then why don't you come cheer your only friend on at his game? I could use all the support I can get."

"You already practically have a fan club around here."

"Yeah, but you being there would mean a lot to me."

"I don't know, Warren..."

"Okay, let me ask you something."

"Depends on what it is." She exercised caution this time, remembering the last time she did that, it hadn't gone so well.

"When was the last time you got out of the house?"

"I wish I could tell you, but now that I think about it...I don't even remember."

"Then what would you say if I asked you to not only come to the game, but to also come to the Spring Fling with me?"

"Now you want me to go to the Spring Fling with you, too?" Jordan's eyebrows arched in amazement.

"I was kind of nervous to ask you sooner. I know it's still a few weeks off and everything."

"Why? It's just me."

"Because I didn't want you to say no, of course." He laughed nervously.

"I would say yes, but I have to check with my parents first. Is that okay?"

"It's cool. Mine are the same way. How about you give me a call after you talk to them tonight?"

He slipped her a folded scrap of paper from between his fingers and left her wishing for another hug as he caressed her hand.

"You're really serious about this?"

"As serious as a heart attack." He winked and

then lifted her hand to his lips, causing Jordan to blush. A warm gust of air blew Jordan's hair away from her face as she watched him leave. She then read and reread the seven digits scrawled on the paper in her hand, and smiled. She could still feel his kiss on her skin, and while they'd joked about a heart attack, her heart was working so hard she was sure she was coming close to experiencing the real thing for herself.

"MOM! I'm home!" Jordan announced her presence as soon as she walked through the door. She wiped the sweat from her forehead with the back of her hand and carelessly tossed her books to the floor. In her excitement, she had run all the way home from the bus stop despite the eighty-degree weather.

"Hey, baby, how was school?" her mother asked over her shoulder as she slid a pan of cake batter into the oven. She had an infamous sweet tooth.

"It was great! I got asked to Spring Fling today!"

"By who?" She had her hands on her hips before Jordan could blink.

"This boy named Warren Taylor." She couldn't contain her smile when she said his name.

"Do I know him?"

"No…but—"

"Then you're not going."

"Mom! How come?" Jordan groaned.

"Because if you're going to be out with some boy, I want to know who he is and what he's about. I'm sure your father would agree," she said as she transferred her used dishes into the sink and rinsed them.

"Okay, well, if you guys meet him and like him, then can I go?"

"We'll see."

"Hey, Riq, wad up? Whatcha doin'?" Jordan walked over to Tariq, who was sitting at the small drop-leaf table by the window. He was hard at work on a sketch, and he didn't bother to look up as she ran her hand over his fresh haircut.

"Drawing."

"Drawing what?"

"A loser," he mumbled with his bottom lip poked out.

"Tariq!" their mother exclaimed at her son's sour attitude. "Why would you draw a something like that?"

"That's me," he said, pointing to the stick figure between vibrant streaks of crayon.

"You're still upset about that game, aren't you?" Jordan asked, remembering the humbling outcome of his latest basketball game. She'd cheered from the bleachers even as his team had formed a line to shake the hands of the winners. The one game he'd won so far this year she'd missed due to her escapade over Jadian Brown.

"I take it he's still upset they lost that game on Saturday?"

"Well, from what I understand, the boys on his new team are blaming the loss on him."

"Why? It's not like he missed the winning shot or something," Jordan said. Kids could be so mean. "He had playtime almost the whole game. He was only on the bench by the fourth quarter."

"They said it was my fault we lost 'cause before I came along, they won their games," Tariq interjected, shaking his head.

"I'm about to call their coach in a minute. I know your father will raise hell for this, but I really think Tariq would be better off just waiting until basketball camp this summer," her mother said, washing her hands and drying them on her apron. "I need to go throw a load in the washer. Can you do me a favor and keep an eye on the oven?" She lifted an overflowing basketful of soiled laundry next to the cellar door and pulled the chain to light the stairwell.

"Sure."

Jordan listened to her mother's house shoes slap against the wooden planks and drummed her fingers on the table in boredom. Her eyes then fell on the cordless telephone next to her. She pulled Warren's number from her pocket and memorized it, knowing that she was only procrastinating. *You've got to tell him, so suck it up and call,* she told herself. After making sure Tariq was still preoccupied, she quickly punched in Warren's number and squeezed her eyes shut as she concentrated on the ringing in her ear.

"May I speak to Warren, please?" She covered her mouth in shock as soon as the words had left her mouth. She couldn't believe she had almost stuttered.

"This him. Who this?"

"Hey, it's me, Jordan."

"Hey, what's up, cutie?" His tone seemed to lighten once he identified her voice on the other end of the line. "I'm glad you called. I hope you have some good news for me."

"I just wanted to let you know that I talked to my mom and she said I can probably go with you to Spring Fling."

"Probably?"

"Well, I won't lie. There is a catch."

"What is it?"

Jordan took a deep breath. "Well, I don't want to freak you out or anything, but my parents want to meet you first."

"Uh-oh, time to meet the parents already?" he joked.

"I know, right." She chuckled uncertainly. Was Warren really okay with this?

"Naw, that's cool, though. When do they want me to come over?"

"How about you come over on Sunday around one?" she asked, unable to believe her luck. Warren was too good to be true. "My mom is going to make Sunday dinner. There's always more than enough food for another spot at the table."

"Sunday at one it is, then. I can't wait." Jordan twirled her hair around her finger and smiled. She couldn't wait, either.

Jordan hummed as she rushed to get the door Sunday afternoon. The doorbell had chimed throughout the house, and Warren was waiting on the porch. She had successfully cleared his invitation to Sunday dinner with her family, and they huddled around the door, eager to meet the first young man who'd come calling for Jordan.

"Hello, how are you doing?" Warren waved and politely addressed her relatives.

"Mom, Dad, this is Warren, and Warren, that's my brother I was telling you about, Tariq. We call him Riq for short." Jordan began to ramble as she played hostess and introduced her guest. She was unsure how to act, and she was afraid he would notice her rattled state. She had never had a boy over to her house before, let alone much interaction with the opposite sex, period.

"Nice to meet you, Warren. I'm Olivia."

"David." Her father extended his hand and gave him a firm handshake. He seemed satisfied by Warren's looking him in the eye, but he only showed it with a huff. Warren was poised, and Jordan admired him for it. Not too many people could look her father in the eye and remain undaunted by the experience.

"Mmm, something smells good," Warren said, sniffing. The scent of a soul food dinner hung in the air.

"You got here just in time. I just took the greens off the stove."

"Don't you want to help me set the table?" Jordan asked as she bravely took Warren by the hand.

"Sure." He allowed her to lead him into the dining

room. She carefully passed him her mother's best china from the hutch as he completed the task without being asked.

"So, what's on the menu?" he inquired while in the middle of proudly examining his work.

"Fried chicken, gizzards—even though I don't eat them. Do you like those?"

"Sure, I eat 'em."

Jordan shuddered before continuing. "Baked mac and cheese, some greens, some sweet potatoes and corn bread."

Just as Jordan described the feast they were sure to enjoy, her mother emerged from the kitchen balancing several serving dishes in her arms.

Warren rushed to her aid. "Here, let me help you with that."

"Oh, you don't have to do that. Thank you." Jordan could tell that her mother was impressed by Warren's manners as she watched him gently set the heaping platters on the table.

"Jordan, go get your father and Tariq." Olivia snapped her fingers and shooed her daughter away.

Jordan returned from retrieving her father and brother from their place in front of the television set to see her mother politely offering a seat to Warren. *So far so good,* she thought.

Jordan scooted her chair closer to the table and caught a flirtatious smile from Warren, who was seated directly across from her. The corners of her mouth turned up only slightly as her father took his place at the head of the table and put his hands out for grace.

"Shall we begin?"

CHAPTER 12

"NO! Don't! Come on, Mom! *Please!* Stop!"

Everyone's laughter tormented Jordan as she desperately tried to snatch the leather photo album from her mother's hands. The night had taken a disastrous turn. One minute, they'd been sitting at the dining room table eating a delicious dinner, and the next, they were being entertained by her intimate baby pictures over brownies à la mode in the living room.

Her mother was quite the storyteller. Jordan glanced around the room to see her brother wiggling in his seat and Warren holding his fist at his mouth to prevent his food from spilling out when he laughed. She rested her head on the armrest of the couch. She had given up on stealing her mother's spot in the limelight. Her mom was thoroughly enjoying her time as the center of attention, and she was using Jordan to do it.

"And here's my little Jordan again. She was only three months old." Olivia leaned closer to Warren and presented him with one of the most embarrassing photographs ever taken of her. Jordan was naked, asleep on a white sheepskin rug.

"Mom!"

"Hey, give that back!" Her mother began cracking up after Jordan escalated her tactics and managed to jump up and retrieve the source of her problem. She hastily creased the photo and stuffed it in her pants pocket.

"Ha, ha, I saw your butt!" Tariq teased.

"Shut up, Riq!"

He stuck his tongue out.

"You two, stop it. We have company." Their mom looked each of them in the eye as she scolded them, but her voice turned sweet when she addressed their guest. "Warren, did you know that Jordan used to call me 'the bestest mommy'? Isn't that adorable!"

"Whatever. She used to be a daddy's girl. I don't know what happened." Her father hadn't said more than a dozen words that evening. He'd been speaking even less to or about Jordan lately, since his discovery of her treachery.

"I think I need some air. Warren, don't you need to be getting home soon?" Jordan's knees were so weak she was barely able to stand as she waited for Warren to catch the hint she was throwing his way. She didn't quite know how to take her father's comment.

"My daughter has no sense of hospitality, does she?" Her mother shook her head and shut the thick collection of priceless memories. "Oh well, you two run along, then. It was such a pleasure having you over today, sweetie. You take care." She gave Warren a tender hug and kissed the air next to each of his cheeks.

"Nice meeting y'all. Thank you for having me. The food was so, *so* good."

"Anytime, anytime." Olivia waved off the compliment as though it meant nothing, but she took great pride in her cooking.

"So you're kicking me out, huh?" Warren kicked loose pebbles along the walkway after Jordan led him outside. She linked her arm in his as she escorted him to his car.

"I can't believe that just happened. I really used to say 'the bestest.'" Jordan was feeling sensitive as she looked back on the embarrassing afternoon. She had always hoped her parents wouldn't pull a stunt like that.

"Aw, it's okay. You were a cute baby." He grinned.

"Yeah, okay."

"Plus, now I can say I saw you naked."

"You're a freak for that one." She giggled.

"How about this? I won't say anything about what just happened in there if you can score *one* basket against me."

Warren stopped at the brand new basketball hoop her father had bought Tariq to lift his spirits about being removed from the rec-and-ed team. He picked up the basketball resting on the lawn and began to dribble it down the limited area of driveway already shared by two vehicles.

"Yeah, right. You have got to be joking." Jordan peered up at the rim as though she were standing next to a giant and then looked down at her girly attire. She scolded herself for trying to look cute for him. Now she didn't stand a chance.

"Come on, one basket ain't nothing. I mean, if you're scared or something…"

"Pass me the ball." She held her hands out and bent her knees to play defense, but without warning, she signaled for a time-out. "Okay, wait."

"What now? The game didn't even start yet and you up here calling a time-out." Warren laughed.

"If I do this, you *swear* you won't tell anybody about what happened in there. *Ever.*"

"All right. Isn't that what I said?"

"Say you *swear.*"

"I promise."

"Pinky promise." She held her curled pinky out to confirm their pact.

"All right, all right." Warren took his time coming near her, and he continued to dribble the ball. Jordan was suspicious of his intentions as she watched him eye the hoop from the corner of his eye. Before she could react, he had charged past her and performed a slam dunk. "Gotcha!"

"You cheater!" Her voice screeched as she watched him swing on the rim.

"Hey, you got to get it how you live," he said as he landed on his feet.

"Don't start nothing you can't finish. I don't want to make you feel bad about yourself." After retrieving the basketball from where it rolled into the grass, she felt confident and powerful with it in her hands.

"Bring it on!"

Her wisecracks provoked him to pass her the ball, and she aggressively tried to drive it to the basket.

Warren was a fierce guard and forced her farther from the hoop, causing their bodies to press against each other. Panicked and greedy for points, Jordan awkwardly hurled the ball at her target.

"Brick!" Warren's curse was paired with the sight of the basketball bouncing off the edge of the metal rim, but giggles coming from the doorway of her home caused him to refocus his energy. "Looks like we have an audience."

"Come here, Riq!" After catching the ball, Jordan looked up to see Tariq standing at the screen door. He had been discreetly watching their game, and Jordan knew he longed to use his over-sized hoop. Their father had had the best intentions when he made the purchase, but Tariq was still too short to touch the rim like his idol, LeBron James.

"Can I play with you guys?"

"Do you want to be on my team?" Warren's voice was kind as he crouched to be level with Tariq.

"Oh, I see how you are. Trying to outnumber me? *Somebody* must feel a little threatened."

"You're still losing, remember?"

"That shot doesn't count!"

"Who says?"

"I do."

"You're making the rules now?"

"Damn right."

"Oooh, you said a bad word!" Tariq teased.

"Shut up before I tell Dad you've been playing with his model cars!"

"Ah, there's nothing like a bond between brother and sister, is there?" Warren sarcastically interjected with a chuckle. Obviously guilty of the crime Jordan had accused him of, Tariq had been silenced in an instant.

"You don't know the half."

"Oh, trust me, I do. I have an older sister out at UCLA. She used to pick on me *all* the time. Does Jordan pick on you, Riq?"

"Mmm-hmm." Tariq folded his skinny arms across his chest with attitude.

"Come here for a second." Warren took Tariq by the shoulder and led him a few feet away. As he whispered something in his ear, Jordan advanced toward the pair. "Ah, ah, ah. No eavesdropping," Warren scolded her.

"Whenever you two are done running your mouths," Jordan taunted the duo as she bounced the ball. Never having been the athletic type, she could barely dribble while standing still, but her mouth ran away with her. "Just say when."

In one simple maneuver, Warren took Tariq in his arms and rushed Jordan for the ball. Tariq's small hands stole it from her almost effortlessly, and Warren lifted him to victory.

"I made it! I dunked like LeBron!" Tariq was full of giggles and smiles as Warren set him on the ground to celebrate.

"Yay! Go, Riq! Go, Riq! Go, Riq, it's your birthday. Give me some love, give me some love."

As Warren and Tariq carried on, Jordan stopped the ball from rolling with her foot. She was undeniably entranced by the heartwarming scene before her as she smoothed her best outfit and used the basketball as an improvised chair. Something in her wanted to smile as she recognized their bond as well as the one forming between her and Warren.

Jordan wobbled and struggled to maintain her balance on the ball, but one charming smile was all it took to replace her fond thoughts with something indescribable. The strange feeling touched her deeply, so deeply its pressures caused her to lose her equilibrium and sent her crashing to the ground. As a concerned Warren rushed her way, she was delirious with laughter. Jordan was falling hard.

* * *

"I didn't wake you up, did I?" Jordan whispered into the phone from where she sat in her window-sill. She could hear the hum of the rain pelting the pavement below as the hours she had left to sleep dwindled away. Tonight, the sky was absent of lightning and without thunder, but the winds were vicious.

"Naw, I'm actually up over here thinking about you." The sound of Warren's voice failed to subdue her wild emotions. She hadn't stopped thinking about him since he'd left.

"Me?"

"Yeah."

"What about me?" Her eyebrows were raised in curiosity, and his deep voice gave her goose bumps.

"I was just thinking about today. It was nice meeting your parents and chillin' with you outside of school. They were cool as hell," he said.

"You just say that because they're not yours. And I thought you said you were thinking about *me?* Tell me what you're thinking about. I can't sleep. I got all night."

"I mean, how can I not be thinking about you. I'm talking to you, ain't I?"

"You know what I mean!"

"Ugh! Why do you do this to me?" His exaggerated laughter faded into a sigh as he tried to hold off his confession. "I was just thinking about how I can't wait to see you at school tomorrow. There, are you happy now?"

"As a matter a fact, I am." She giggled.

"Yeah, yeah, don't get a big head. But what about you? What are you doing up so late? It's already a quarter to two," he said. Jordan could hear him flipping through television channels in search of something good to watch. "Be for real, I know you're over there fantasizing about me. Admit it." His irresistible tone had Jordan on her feet. She bit her lip; her body temperature was up. She began to pace the room, anticipating the topics their conversation was bound to explore that night, until a high-pitched beep rang in her ear.

"Dammit! My phone is about to die." She was annoyed by the flashing battery symbol on the screen.

Warren barely had time to say good-night before the caller ID screen went black. Jordan sighed and lazily dropped the phone on the floor beside her bed before rolling over. She felt awkward for lying there beaming, but she was overjoyed, and she couldn't stop no matter how hard she tried. She closed her eyes and struggled to fall asleep as images of Warren flooded her thoughts. He seemed like everything she could ever ask for in a boyfriend, but she had never viewed him in such a way before out of respect for her friendship with Adrienne.

Now, with Adrienne out of the way and with her parents' approval, she was free to feel any way she wanted. She couldn't deny that she had developed a serious crush on Warren Taylor, and something made her think he might reciprocate her feelings. The line between them had died that night, but Jordan knew she'd made a new connection.

CHAPTER 13

"Jordan! Hurry up! We're already running late!" Olivia was hollering to be heard over the stereo, but Jordan ignored her. Seconds later, she jumped and spun around when she heard the door to her room open. Her mother stood in the doorway. She hadn't bothered to knock, and she pointed her finger toward the floor as a signal to lower the music.

Jordan was on the verge of a breakdown as she paced her room barefoot. She was only half-dressed, her hair was still wet from her shower, and discarded clothes seemed to cover every surface.

"What's wrong? I thought you said the game started at seven? Why aren't you ready yet?"

"Because..." she whined, "I don't have anything to wear!"

Jordan dropped to her bed in hopelessness. Her mother put her hands on her hips and studied the length of the room.

"Jordan, if you don't throw something on... You've got plenty of cute stuff. Here. What about this?" Her mother handed her a white strapless top with a black belt that wrapped around the stomach. "And what's wrong with those pants you got on?"

"Nothing, I guess." Jordan twisted her mouth as she stood and evaluated her choice in the mirror.

"See that. Now all you really need is some cute shoes. How about those black pumps you have? I've never really seen you wear them." Olivia moved a small pile of clothes to the side and took a seat on the edge of Jordan's bed.

"Oh! I forgot all about those. Thank you!" Jordan didn't hesitate to grab the peep-toe heels from the bottom of her closet. She was a big fan of sneakers and usually found the labor involved in wearing heels to be bothersome. But tonight she was willing to make an exception. She wanted to make sure she looked exceptional for Warren.

As she took a seat on the floor to slide on her shoes, her mother began brushing her hair. Jordan was relaxed by the soothing strokes, and she felt silly for having gotten so upset.

"So, Warren can really ball, right? You're not having me sit up here with you at this game if he's a bench rider."

"What! You were the one who wanted to come. And for your information, Warren has scouts coming to this game tonight." Jordan was caught off guard by her mother's words, and by the hint of pride she felt.

"Oooh, you sure told me, didn't you? Aha, Jordan's got a crush," her mother teased.

"Mom! No, I don't!"

"Yes, you do. I can tell."

Her mother opened a jar of moisturizer and rubbed it through Jordan's hair. She parted the hair and made two smooth French braids on each side. After a quick inspection in a hand mirror, Jordan quickly got back on her feet and hurried to her dresser.

She rubbed peach-flavored lip gloss on her lips and pulled an eyelash curler out of the top drawer.

"Uh-uh, look at you. You know you don't need that. You got those good eyelashes like Mommy."

"Whatever."

"Don't brush me off. I spent nine months making you. I want to admire my work."

Jordan just shook her head and closed her eyes as she let the fresh peach scent of one of her favorite body sprays fall on her skin. She opened her eyes and turned toward her mother.

"How do I look?"

Her mother waved her hand to fan the mist away from her nose.

"You look very pretty."

"Mom! When are we leaving?" Tariq sounded as though he'd used all his might to project his tiny voice from the bottom of the stairs.

"In a minute, Tariq!" Olivia yelled. "Wow, look who's more excited to go to this game than you," she whispered to Jordan.

"Nah, I don't know about that."

"So I take it you're finally ready?"

"As ready as I'll ever be."

Jordan pushed the limit of how fast she could walk in her heels as she made her way to the school entrance. Her mother and Tariq were right behind her, hand in hand. Tariq was practically skipping, he wanted so badly to see a basketball game played by the "big kids," especially Warren.

As the ticket taker at the door stamped their hands for admission, Jordan scanned the crowd for a place to sit. It was a packed house tonight, and they'd arrived during halftime.

Olivia tucked her change in her purse as Jordan led the way to a cramped space courtside. They quickly hustled over to the bleachers and those already seated were kind enough to scoot over and make more room.

Jordan violently chewed a now flavorless piece of gum she'd bribed from Tariq while she stared at the entrance the players would return from. The cheerleading squad revved up the crowd, generating more anticipation and thirst for a home victory. Loyal supporters had their cheeks painted with the school's colors, and they had the floor shaking from pounding their feet.

Jordan watched the group of cheerleaders scamper from center court with wide, exaggerated smiles held tight on their faces. The applause was beginning to die, and her mother leaned over to speak to her. She was only on her first word when the applause came back to life and the stands broke out in an uproar.

Jordan was torn away from her mother's message, and she stood to see the teams reentering the gym, more than ready to finish the game. Jordan spotted Warren and screamed his name for him to hear her. She tried to mask her surprise when he actually acknowledged her with a wave and sprinted over to her.

"I thought you weren't going to make it." Warren was overwhelmed with adrenaline. He stared admiringly at Jordan before forcing himself to greet her family. He extended his hand for a low five from Tariq as he said, "Hi, Mrs. Wright, Riq. Nice ya'll could make it."

"Hey there, yourself. Good luck out there."

"You better go." Jordan spotted Coach Avery's eyes burning into Warren's neck and nodded his way.

"I know. Good luck." She could hear the crowd shouting out his name and number everywhere around her when she stood and fearlessly planted a kiss on his cheek.

The crowd let out a round of "aws," and Jordan reclaimed her seat, laughing and growing hot with embarrassment. Warren arrogantly played up their moment and motioned the crowd to keep it up. Jordan didn't take her eyes off him as he ran to the other end of the court. His jersey flowed in the wind, and his muscular arms were highlighted by his glistening sweat.

Jordan hoped for some time alone with him tonight. She looked over at her mother and brother and weighed her chances. Her father was out tonight, playing poker with his friends. She just wanted a chance to get to know Warren away from school *and* her parents.

Jordan glanced at the scoreboard for a moment, and the buzzer sounded. The countdown for the final thirty-odd seconds of the game had begun. The score was 62–62. Apparently the Hornets had made quite a few improvements since the last time they'd squared off, and Warren looked exhausted from carrying the team. He'd scored more than half of their points.

Jordan held her breath as she watched him dash from the sideline and down the court. She bit her nails as she watched him pass the ball to another player to slip by a block set up for him. Not even one second later Warren signaled for the ball and gracefully received it. He was ready to take it to the hole and go out with a bang by winning the game with a slam dunk, but time was running out. He opted not to show off, but when he went to go inside, he had men guarding him from every angle to lock him down.

The screams and cheers coming from the stands faded, and Warren jumped as high as he could and shot the ball. His Jordans landed on the three-point line, and he held his pose until the basketball swooshed through the net.

"Warren Taylor with the jumper! And he makes it! I've never seen anything like it! Number five wins the game for the team!"

The announcer continued to have a fit over the PA system, and the school gym erupted into wild celebration. Fans rushed the mirrorlike hardwood floor, but Jordan stuck close to her mother as the rowdy crowd swallowed Warren and then lifted him high enough for everyone to see. They sat him on their shoulders as if they were placing him on a throne.

Jordan sought to make eye contact because she was afraid to brave the crowd and get closer to him. Warren was breathing hard, but he never stopped smiling and releasing his energy through victorious yells. His team surrounded him with praise, and others with congratulations. He continued to listen as he wiped his dripping face with a small hand towel tossed his way, and his eyes continuously searching below him.

Jordan stood with her hands cupped together, impatiently wanting to congratulate him on his win. She was on the tips of her toes so fast she came close to jumping clear off the ground. Warren was looking directly at her and blew her a kiss that could've knocked her over in her awestruck condition.

"Jordan, we need to get going to beat all this

traffic. Your brother needs to get home and get to bed," Olivia said.

"But I want to say hi to Warren first," Tariq moaned as his arm hung weakly from his mother's hand. He'd had an active day of playing in the sun, and what small reserve of energy he'd had left had been drained over the course of the game.

"Well, I'm in no mood to deal with these crazy people and their driving, Tariq. You're just going to have to talk to him later."

"Mom?" Jordan looked down at the floor when posing her question.

"Yeah?"

"Do you mind if I stay?" she asked, lagging behind.

"How are you going to get home?"

"I'll ask Warren to drop me off. I'm sure he wouldn't mind."

"Does he have his license?"

"Yes, Mom."

"All right, you can stay. But I expect you in by midnight and not a second later. Don't test me, Jordan. I'm not even playing with you."

"Okay, Mom. I promise I'll be home by twelve." Jordan knew why her mother was so testy and did her best to reassure her that she was still trustworthy.

"Okay. Have fun. I love you." Jordan could slightly feel her mother's acrylic nails on her scalp as she pulled her close and kissed her on the cheek.

"I love you, too. Bye, Riq."

"Twelve o'clock."

Jordan turned her back on her mother's warning to search for Warren all over again in the diminishing crowd. She had just begun to feel disappointment sinking in when a pair of firm arms grabbed her from behind and hugged her. Warren pecked the nape of her neck and she whirled around to see him face-to-face.

"Oh my God, you were amazing! What did the scouts say? Anything?"

"I don't know. I'll have to see what they say, wait until they talk to Coach."

"Oh. Well, anyway, you did so good! I'm so proud of you!"

"Thank you." He paused and looked around. "Where'd everybody go?" he asked in reference to Olivia and Tariq.

"Oh. They went home. I hope you're not mad, but I said you'd give me a ride back."

"It's cool. What time you got to be in?"

"Twelve."

"A'ight. Well, let me go change and we can be out. Give me ten minutes."

"Okay."

"Here are my keys. You can wait for me in my whip if you want."

"Okay, it's the silver Impala, right?" Jordan toyed with the keys in her hand, and just when she'd gotten the question out of her mouth, a rambunctious friend of Warren's interrupted them to share the win and approve of Warren's performance.

"Ahh! My nigga Warren was killin' them niggas!"

Warren gave a quick nod, giving Jordan the go-ahead, and watched her walk away. Jordan turned to face him again, holding his eyes as she backed out of the gym. She liked the way he was looking at her, watching her hips sway back and forth.

"Ay! Hello! You all there?" His friend, Marlon, was waving his hands inches from his face.

Warren suddenly shook his head and grinned at Jordan, flashing ten fingers and mouthing, "Ten minutes."

She smiled back and walked out the door, allowing Warren to reply. Whenever Jordan was in his presence, it was as though no one else existed at that moment.

CHAPTER 14

Jordan sat patiently for an extra five minutes as she thumbed through Warren's book-like CD case. The overhead light went on, and Jordan turned to see Warren toss his duffel bag on the backseat and take his place behind the wheel. As he turned the key in the ignition, he immediately started seeking a track on the CD currently playing. He settled for "Wonder Woman" by Trey Songz, and by the time the first verse came on, the school was in his rearview mirror.

Warren let down all the windows and opened the sunroof to get some relief from the humidity. The sky was nearly covered in lavender clouds, but the moon still shone brightly, never permanently obscured.

"So, what are you trying to get into tonight?" he asked casually.

"I don't know. It's already a little late. I just wanted to get away from the house for a minute."

"I feel you."

"How are you so calm right now? If I were you I wouldn't know *what* to do." Jordan found his court skills to be jaw-dropping.

"Man, I'm just tryin' to chill and reflect on things. Shit, I know I'm definitely trying to spend my time with you. What made you want to come chill with me tonight?"

"I don't know," she lied with a shrug. She thought it best to keep her feelings inside, and stiffened when trying to come up with scenarios in which she could tell him she cared about him.

"Whatever it was, I'm happy you did. But before we do anything, do you care if we run by my crib real fast? I just need to hop in the shower right quick. I promise I won't take long."

"Okay, as long as you feed me after that. I'm starving."

"See, now, that's what I'm talking about! I'm hungry as hell. Don't you try and front by ordering a salad and shit either."

"Shut up!" She playfully smacked him in the arm and laughed. She rubbed her lips together to spread the small amount of gloss left on her lips and made sure the tips of her braids were still in place on her shoulders.

"Damn," Warren said, turning his head to look at her.

"Warren, watch the road!" Jordan screamed as the car began to drift into the oncoming lane. They were lucky there was no traffic.

"Why are you trippin'!" Warren asked as he steered the car back inside the lines in the road.

"Because! You're up here swerving all over the place with your non-driving self!"

"My bad, but you're going to have to stop doing that." He chuckled.

"Doing what? I didn't do anything!"

"Yes, you did. It's your fault. You distracted me," he joked.

"I distracted you how? You're full of it!" Jordan was worked up, and laughed along.

"'Cause, man, you're just sitting over there looking so good, I can't stop myself from just…looking at you. You don't know how many times I had to catch myself during the game. I thought you weren't even going to come at first, but then I saw you and—" He looked over at the passenger seat and Jordan bashfully smiled back. "Ha. I've said too much," he said, weakly laughing at himself.

They cruised down the street, then came to a stop sign. He rested his arm behind the headrest of her seat and looked deep into her eyes when he spoke. "Stop being so scared and just relax. Ain't nothing bad going to happen. You trust me?"

Jordan didn't hesitate to say yes, and Warren tested her by pulling off and holding their stare. He did so only for a few seconds, and Jordan remained calm. Once he reached the entrance to an upper-middle-class housing complex, he zoomed for his house. Jordan noticed the darkened interior as they sat facing an opening garage door, and focused on the music.

Jordan's mind went into overdrive as the door hit concrete behind the car. Warren had his bag out of the backseat before she had even opened her door. He could tell she was concerned as he turned his key in the lock.

"My parents are out of town until next week."

"Oh? Where are they?" she asked, her eyes wandering to take in her new surroundings.

"In Vegas."

"Aren't you mad they went without you? I know I would be."

"No. I chose to stay here. I didn't want to fall behind and miss games."

"Then I take it you're not mad they weren't at your game?"

"As long ago as I started doing this, I don't expect them to make all my games anymore. Maybe a few here and there, but it really doesn't bother me. I just go out there and do what I do."

"So...what'd they go to Vegas for?"

"They went out there to celebrate their twenty-fifth anniversary."

"Dang, my parents haven't even been married *that* long," Jordan said, studying a large family portrait hanging on the living room wall.

"So, are you cool chillin' down here while I go ahead and get in the shower? Do you want something to drink or anything?"

"No. I'm fine."

"A'ight." Warren hustled upstairs, and within seconds, Jordan could hear water running. She took a seat on the couch and searched for the remote to the big-screen television, but after finding it, she found she didn't know how to operate it. Time was passing so slowly it pained Jordan to keep still any longer. She started to give in to her mounting curiosity to explore Warren's home, and before she knew it one foot was on the bottom stair, and then two.

The door to his bedroom was wide-open, but she

decided to leave it open just an inch. She was immediately fascinated with his room. She carefully moved about, and she respectfully admired his things as though she were at a museum. He had a shrine of trophies and ribbons on his wall to back up his history and talent with the sport of basketball. His room was sophisticated and mature in its design—each piece of furniture matched and a Ralph Lauren comforter set was smoothed neatly across his bed. His room not only looked like it came straight from the pages of a catalog, it was clean like it, too.

Satisfied with what she'd uncovered, she headed for the door, pausing when she noticed a photo of Warren and a girl she guessed was his older sister in Halloween costume. He must have been only three or so when the picture was taken. He was chubby, and he looked miserable in his bulky pumpkin costume, but Jordan found it strangely cute.

"Ha, ha. This is payback!" She could feel a burning sensation in her sides from laughing so hard, but she nearly choked when Warren suddenly entered.

"Do you like my room?"

"I'm sorry...I was just...um..." Jordan fumbled with the frame as she returned it to its rightful place on the dresser. She'd been so busy with the picture she hadn't even noticed that the water was no longer running.

"Oh, I see you found my favorite picture," he said, tossing a black Dickies set onto his bed from his closet.

"Sorry. I know I shouldn't be in here. I shouldn't have touched anything."

"Stop apologizing. Do I look mad to you?" Warren's skin was still wet from the shower, and his curly hair sparkled with drops of water. Jordan's mouth went dry when she let her eyes follow droplets down his toned chest to the hand holding a towel low around his defined waist.

"What were you looking for, other girls' phone numbers or something?" he asked while continuing to coordinate his outfit.

"That doesn't even make any sense. Why would I be looking for phone numbers?" She was trying to mask her emotions, but she knew how well she was doing.

"I don't know. Maybe you were looking for something you don't want to find." He twirled his finger in a circular motion, gesturing for her to turn around. She started when she heard his heavy cotton towel fall to the rug. He was only a few feet away from her back.

"There shouldn't be anything to find, though, that's the whole point. And what makes you think you know so much about me?" Jordan shot back, struggling to keep her voice steady.

"Well, there's not, and I never said I did. I was just sharing an observation."

Jordan kept her eyes on the floor as she listened to Warren get dressed. She wanted to take back what she'd said. "Well…it's whatever….I really don't care." She folded her arms across her chest and stared blankly at the wall. She wouldn't dare turn around until she was sure he was ready, but the idea to do so prematurely had popped up more than a few times. The racy image she'd worked up in her mind made her body shake.

"Still, just to let you know…there's nothing to find."

Jordan turned around to see Warren standing directly in front her and looking fine in perfectly pressed shorts, a crisp white tee and jacket. He covered the goose bumps on her arms as he rubbed them for warmth. He stared into her eyes to convey his seriousness before extending his hand toward the door, motioning for her to lead the way.

Over a platter of chicken strips and french fries at a local waffle house, Jordan threw her head back and burst into a fit of laughter for what felt like the hundredth time that night. She appreciated Warren's not trying to make a move on her at his house and remaining a gentleman. It seemed that there were no catches with him—he really was a great guy.

Jordan picked up another french fry from the dish they shared, and Warren watched her, smiling widely. "I know I never told you this, but you have the funniest laugh I've ever heard."

Jordan acted as though she was about to throw a fry his way and giggled when he dodged nothing. She washed down the potatoes with a sip of soda, and then made sure to reestablish eye contact right away in an effort not to be distracted by his good looks. Sitting so close to him, knowing he was watching her every move, Jordan was nervous and elated in equal measure.

"Tell me, do you believe the things Adrienne told people about me?" she asked, suddenly feeling bold.

"I thought that was pretty obvious by now," Warren replied.

"Hey, you never know. I just don't want you to get the impression that I'm easy, because I'm not," she said firmly.

"If I thought you were easy, I would've been trying

to fuck you, Jordan." Jordan's eyes grew large, and she was openmouthed at his blunt language.

"Well, you want it straight, don't you?" Warren chuckled. "All I'm saying is, if I was just trying to hit, you would know. I just had the perfect opportunity to seduce you, *if* I'd wanted to."

"Seduce me? You sound like a lame soap opera." Her laughing soon ceased and her brow furrowed. "Why didn't you?"

"Because, *maybe* I like you and I want to get to *know* you, make sure you're not just messin' with me to get back at Adrienne." He was being a bit of a smart aleck, but Jordan could tell he meant what he said. He noisily stabbed at the ice in the bottom of his cup with his straw.

"And *maybe* I like you, too…" Her smile vanished. "But can you say you noticed me before? Things used to be…different." She left her comment vague, not wanting to paint a vivid picture of her former self. As she posed her question, her eyes probed his, and his warm hands softly caressed hers.

"I've always noticed you. Adrienne got in the way of me getting to you sooner."

"How so? I mean, I know once she said she was feelin' you, I looked the other way. But that was still your decision to give in to her."

"And that's my mistake. But that don't mean nothing and this isn't about her or anybody else. This is about us."

"We're here. Right on time." Warren's car came to a stop in front of Jordan's house. It was quarter to twelve, which meant she had at least fifteen minutes to spare.

"Thank you so much. I had a lot of fun." Her voice was groggy, and she clutched a white styrofoam carton of dessert to go.

"Yeah, me, too. Do you want me to walk you to your door?"

She didn't hesitate to answer. "No. That's okay." She had to avoid a good-night kiss, even though she fantasized about what it would be like. It wasn't that she wasn't open to something as innocent as a kiss, she just didn't know how.

"What's wrong with you? You're cold again? I don't even have the air-conditioning on," Warren said, noting another wave of goose bumps. "Here. How about this?" He took off his jacket and draped it over her shoulders. "Better?"

"Yeah, thanks."

"Can I call you tomorrow when I get home from practice?"

"Sure. I'd like that." She smiled, her hand already on the door handle.

And that was when it came. The moment she had been sure she steered clear of. Warren's eyes were lower than usual, and an uncomfortable silence only added to the pressure. Jordan held her breath as Warren leaned in for a kiss with his eyes closed, and in her distress she jumped out of the car and slammed the door before he could reach her.

"Good night!" she called to him over her shoulder as she shuffled across the street, nearly falling on her face. She had her key ready when she reached the door, and as she turned it in the lock, she looked back to see Warren pulling off looking confused. She sighed and stepped into the house, knowing she faced a sleepless night ahead.

CHAPTER 15

"Isn't this one hell of a way to start my week! What does he see in her, anyway?" Adrienne grumbled. She was leaning on Michelle's locker, only feet away from where Jordan and Warren stood. Classes hadn't started for the day, and the two were openly flirting.

Standing around Adrienne, Farrah, Kenya and Michelle were discussing their plans for the night of Spring Fling, describing their outfits to each other in painstaking detail. Adrienne's nonstop trash-talking was causing Farrah to miss some vital details, and she was tired of straining to hear.

"Ugh! Oh my God, Adrienne, that shit is *too* old! Life moves on," she hissed over Adrienne's shoulder.

"What's wrong now?" Michelle sighed.

Farrah nodded toward Jordan and Warren, who

were doing nothing but talking at his locker. He stood in front of Jordan, his back to the crowd and his hands pressed against the wall around her face. He would occasionally whisper something in Jordan's ear that would make her laugh, but to anyone but Adrienne the scene was no big deal.

"I wish I would be stuck on some nigga. Warren ain't even all that cute." Kenya turned her nose up in the air in disapproval. She was growing tired of Adrienne's endless interruptions which always brought up the same old topic.

"For real, Adrienne, hop up off Jordan's nuts. We don't like the bitch, either, but you don't see us up here talking about her all the time day and fucking night, do you?" Michelle snapped.

"Whatever," Adrienne said glumly.

"So it's time to let it go. Who cares if they're together now? What, you're not still messing with Maurice?" Farrah more said than asked, as though she already knew the answer.

"No. I am. We're going to Spring Fling together." It hurt Adrienne to turn away from the budding couple she was trying to destroy, but she forced herself to face her friends. She knew Jordan liked Warren; why she hadn't seen it all along, she wasn't sure. Now she knew that even though she'd found a new man, her feelings for Warren meant that Maurice didn't really stand a chance.

Bitterly, Adrienne remembered the way Maurice had looked at Jordan in the hallway all those mornings ago. Jordan hadn't even noticed, but the attraction in his eyes hadn't escaped Adrienne. As soon as his girlfriend, Sandra, had called it quits, girls had started lining up at his door. But he hadn't been seeing anyone regularly, and there were few whispers about his even talking to anyone more than once.

Adrienne had pulled it off and snagged Maurice for herself, and she felt that she held a small victory over Jordan. Her joy hadn't lasted long, though. What she'd just seen blew her so-called accomplishment out of the water. And to make matters worse, Adrienne had given it up to Maurice on the first date, just to seal the deal. But when she mentioned a relationship, he tried to put her off with an adventurous tale of "secret lovers" keeping their rendezvous on the "down-low."

Impatient with his games, she'd insisted he take her to the Spring Fling, and he'd reluctantly agreed. "He asked me a couple of days ago," she said.

"Hmm, that's not what I heard." Michelle faked her concern to mask her teasing.

"And what the hell is that supposed to mean, Michelle?"

"Never mind." She sighed. "I'm about to go to the bathroom."

She announced where she was going as though it were important. Kenya, Farrah and a very reluctant Adrienne followed like sheep. It was a rule to never go anywhere without the other girls in their exclusive circle.

"Wait." Michelle stopped Adrienne in her tracks. "Adrienne, could you stay here and watch my locker for me? You know my lock is broken."

"But…it's been that way all week." Edison Junior High Library

"I know."

She and her friends walked off, laughing and undoubtedly talking about Adrienne.

Adrienne felt neglected as she stood alone at their designated territory in the hallway. At first she thought she was glad to be rid of the distraction, but in no time the loneliness set in, and to hide her hurt feelings about being abandoned, she was beginning to display signs of her temper. Nothing could distract her from keeping tabs on her exes now.

Yet, as angry as she was, Jordan and Warren were oblivious. She was becoming more heated by the second as she watched Jordan having a good time.

She hoped the bell would ring any minute, but time seemed to drag. She knew that if she didn't cool down soon there was going to be trouble, and she was sent over the edge when Jordan handed over what she assumed to be a gift.

It was just Warren's size, and she laughed at Jordan. She was tricking on Warren, and that was why he was acting the way he was. Adrienne was sure she had it all figured out now, and wondered why she hadn't thought of that possibility sooner herself. If it was all a scam, there was hope she and Warren could give things another try. She would do anything to make him happy, but for whatever reason, he couldn't see that.

However, when Warren put his hand up to refuse the jacket and made Jordan put it on, Adrienne's jaw dropped to the floor. She could feel her heart breaking beneath her anger as she watched Jordan turn to admire it in the mirror hanging on the door of his locker. Adrienne sucked her teeth at Jordan's appearance. It still blew her mind how the two people she'd once held so close to her heart had gone on to find love and happiness. She couldn't understand how they could be so content without her. Warren actually wanted her, Jordan Wright, of all the girls in school, to rock his clothes for everyone to see.

Adrienne recognized that he was staking a kind of claim on Jordan by giving her his jacket, and she had had enough. After all, Adrienne was the true victim in this situation. Warren had used her for a "favor" and dissed her after it was all said and done, moving on to her best friend?

Adrienne used the last of her lip gloss before approaching them and swallowed hard before tapping Warren on his shoulder. This was the ultimate test, but if she could get Warren to ignore Jordan and pay attention to her, even if for a moment, it would be worth it.

"Hey, boo, how you been? I haven't talked to you in forever. What, you don't know nobody no more?" Warren looked disappointed to turn around and see her. She played up a false, sultry tone when greeting him, but she shot Jordan an intimidating once-over from head to toe and rolled her eyes. "Jordan."

Jordan's jaw was tight, and she ignored Adrienne's greeting.

"What do you want, Adrienne? I know you saw us over here talking," Warren said.

"Why do you have to be so fucking rude? I ain't do nothing to your ass!" Adrienne snapped.

"Hey, I'm about to go," Jordan whispered, but Warren pressed his hand against her.

"Naw, hold up."

"And, you! I should fuck your ass up!" Adrienne's voice rose to a rage-filled scream, and she grabbed for Jordan like a wild woman.

"Uh-uh, you better get the hell on with that fighting shit." Warren puffed his chest out, bumping Adrienne back a step as he shielded Jordan by standing between them.

Adrienne knew he was not going to move, and unlike Jordan, she hadn't been at all surprised when he'd come to Jordan's defense. The two girls locked eyes for a moment, and when the bell rang, a small group of curious onlookers hung behind. Clearly embarrassed, Adrienne broke their stare and took off down the hall. Jordan moved to pursue her, but Warren grabbed her by the hand before she could get far. He led her in the other direction, a soft kiss on the cheek serving as a worthwhile distraction, but a distraction nonetheless.

The sun was beating down on Jordan's back as she searched for her bus. Beads of sweat were already beginning to form on her forehead, and she'd only been exposed to the stifling heat for mere seconds.

As she continued to make her way past the rows

of buses, she toyed with the straps of her book bag. She couldn't stop thinking about the performance Adrienne had put on that morning. She couldn't help wondering what would've happened if Adrienne had gotten ahold of her. What if Warren hadn't been there? What would Adrienne have done?

Nevertheless, she didn't want to dwell on Adrienne's escalating threats. Neither one of them had gotten into a fistfight their entire lives. Not even Adrienne with her smart mouth. She'd always had the bad habit of speaking before she thought, and she'd somehow managed to avoid the consequences all these years.

Beep! Beep!

At the sound of the horn, Jordan turned to see Warren cruising slowly beside her.

"Ay! You want a ride home?" he called to her over his music, and gestured for her to come along with a wave of his hand. "Get in."

Jordan hurried around his silver car to the passenger-side door. A slight breeze blew his lightweight oversized jacket against her legs. Warren tried to brush off his sexual thoughts, but catching a flash of her denim shorts every once in a while was the only thing that made her not appear naked underneath.

"No practice today?" Jordan asked, clicking on her seat belt. Warren sped off right away and rolled up the passenger-side window to trap the air-conditioning. As the vent blew out a cool breeze, Jordan took a deep breath of relief.

"Nope, not today. Whatchu got up?"

"I don't know. Nothing, really. I'll probably just go home and chill, do my homework, eat, sleep… You know, the usual."

"A'ight, but how about you do something *un*-usual? I got something we can do that's way better than what you're talking about."

"What is it?"

"There's this carnival going on. The only thing is, it's all the way on the other side of town. I rode by it the other day and I want to go see if it's poppin'."

"Oh, that sounds fun! Let me see your phone for a second?" She held up a hand to catch the razor-thin phone and punched in her phone number. She bit her lip when she saw that her number was programmed into his phone under the catchy nickname "J-Baby."

She was giddy while listening to the ringing on the other end of the line. Her mom was sure to answer, and after having already allowed her to hang out with Warren after his basketball game, Jordan assumed she would say yes to this minor request.

"Hello? Wright residence."

"Hey...um...Daddy. Is Mom there?" Jordan started stumbling over her words, and her eyes widened when she heard her father's low voice. He had a voice big enough for a giant, and at his height, it was fitting.

"No, she's not. She had to take Tariq to the dentist and she's still not back yet. What number are you calling me from? Shouldn't you be on your way home?"

"Yeah. I'm on Warren's cell phone. I was calling to ask if me and him could go to this carnival across town. I don't know the name of it exactly, but he said he passed it while driving and wanted to see what all they had."

"I know which one he's probably talking about, but I don't know about you going out there tonight. It's a school night, so you have to get up early. I don't want you giving your mom a hard time waking you up in the morning."

"Come on, Daddy. Please, please, Daddy? *Please?* I swear on everything I'll get up on time for school tomorrow," she begged.

"Okay, as long as you're in by eight-thirty. Do you have a lot of homework?"

"No." Jordan crossed her fingers when she lied to

her father. She in fact had an English paper due the next morning, but for Warren she'd put it aside. It would just have to wait.

"All right. Have fun."

"Oh, thank you, Daddy! Bye! I love you!" she squealed. She folded the cell phone and turned to Warren. "I have good news." She grinned.

"What's that?" He only glanced at her for a split second before he refocused on the road ahead and continued to navigate their way to the carnival.

"You have me to yourself for the next five whole hours!" She shot up in her seat with an excitement in her eyes she couldn't hide, and gave his hand a loving squeeze.

Time was flying by for Jordan and Warren, but they'd had a ton of fun. They had walked the dirt lot holding hands the entire time they were there, until Warren won Jordan a huge stuffed Tweety bird from one of the many games on either side of the main walkway.

As dusk fell upon the city, the carnival came alive with bright, colorful lights and festive music. The various aromas coming from the food stands became stronger, but the smell of cotton candy seemed to dominate the air. They still had an hour and a half to spend together, but the crowd had swelled and was much larger than when they had arrived. With the lines to the rides becoming longer and longer, they decided to head back to Warren's house. Not that either of them was disappointed. They'd had a chance to ride each attraction they wanted more than once.

"Oh, no. Wait, wait, wait. We have to ride this." Jordan yanked on Warren's hand to stop him. She peered to the top of the Ferris wheel and allowed another handful of fluffy pink cotton candy to melt in her mouth.

"Man, let's go. We rode all the rides here a million times."

"But not this one. How could we have missed this? It's the classic carnival ride."

"Who says?"

"I don't know… Me. Everybody." She stopped for a moment. "Wait a minute. I know Warren Taylor's not scared to get on some slow-ass Ferris wheel."

"It's not about the speed." The dread he felt came across in what he said as he looked up at the wheel rotating high into the sky.

"Aw, you're scared of heights?" Jordan cooed as she wrapped her arm around his.

"Can't even fuck with 'em."

"Come on, now. I've seen bigger. It's doesn't even look like its a hundred feet up!"

"Well, you sure could've fooled me. And you tell me the difference. I don't care if its one hundred feet or two hundred feet, no matter how you put it, it's still too high!"

"I'm *going* to ride this ride before we leave."

"A'ight, you go right ahead and do that. Me and Tweety will be waiting for you right here when you get off." He used one of the stuffed wings to wave goodbye. "Bye!"

"That's not going to cut it and you know it," Jordan said, folding her arms.

"How'd I get stuck holding this big-ass thing anyway? I'm the one who won it for you." He held the stuffed animal up in the air for inspection in an attempt to change the topic.

"All right, here, give it to me." She snatched her gift and put a pitiful pout on her face. "I'll just ride the Ferris wheel with Tweety. *He's* brave enough to ride it with me."

"You expect that to work?" He tried to resist the pleading look in her eyes but failed miserably. Before he knew it, she was leading him to the line. "Okay, man, damn! Let's just get this over with."

They found a seat, and an attendant confiscated

the large prize until after the ride was over. Warren looked nauseated as the small bench swung back and forth.

"Oooh, scary!" Jordan mocked him with big eyes when they began to move. She couldn't help laughing at the expression on his face.

"Say bye to Tweety!" She waved to the yellow cartoon character growing smaller as they went higher. As she leaned forward, their seat started to rock, and Warren grabbed her arm.

"Jordan, stop! That shit ain't funny! Are you trying to kill us?" He pulled her back from over the bar positioned across their laps.

"What's wrong with you? You act like I'm going to just fall out," Jordan joked, leaning over the side once again.

"Oh my God." Warren sighed nervously and used his hand like a visor to shield his eyes.

"Okay, I'm going to stop messing with you." She chuckled and sat back in her seat.

"Right, while you're up here being all mean, you're missing out on a big opportunity."

"To do what?"

"Hold me. 'Cause I'm scared." Warren jokingly changed the pitch of his voice, and Jordan opened her arms to him. She laughed softly as she wrapped her arms around his body and he rested his head on her chest.

"You are too much."

They sat in silence, enjoying their ride as their bench brought them back to the world they'd come from and away again. Jordan let out a gasp when the operator stopped the ride, with them at the very top.

"You've got to be kidding me," Warren said, looking pale.

"Uh-oh, look at us stuck at the top! This is the best part! Look at this view!"

"Hell naw." Warren seemed like he was going to lose it at any second. He kept his composure by keeping his head low and shielding his eyes with his hands. In her excitement, Jordan sent them swaying back and forth once again.

"It's so peaceful up here. Look at all them down there, and you can barely hear them." She peered over the side of their seat and paused only for a moment before gazing up at the night sky.

"Ooh! Look how close we are to the moon tonight! And look up at the stars…they're so beautiful. It looks like you can almost reach out and touch one, doesn't it? I wish I—"

It took Jordan a minute to realize Warren's lips

were actually touching hers. Her eyes were still open at first, but once he began to gently suck on her lips, she let go of the anxiousness that had initially left her frozen. She allowed herself to shut her eyes as well, and relaxed enough to let Warren guide her in returning his kisses.

Jordan couldn't believe what was happening, and she prayed she was doing it right, whatever that really meant. She had never imagined when she woke up that today would be the day she would have her first kiss. Not that she had any objections.

His lips were so soft she couldn't think of anything to compare them to, and she didn't want to stop kissing him until she could at least describe them better. The way he took his time kissing her and the way he made her feel when he did it left her mesmerized. Jordan might not have been able to touch the stars tonight, but she still felt as if she were on top of the world.

CHAPTER 16

NOt even half an hour later, Jordan had gone from feeling on top of the world to having Warren on top of her. They jetted for his place as soon as the ride came to a stop, and ever since, they had lain kissing passionately for what felt like hours.

They tumbled around on his couch, kissing and touching each other throughout their make-out session. Jordan loved the feeling of Warren's hands all over her body and beneath her shirt. She closed her eyes when she felt him kiss her neck. She was in another state. As he traveled between her lips and her neck, his fingers worked to undo her jeans, and she didn't resist.

Her moans created a vibrating sensation against his lips as he pushed his fingers deeper into her lace-trimmed panties. Having never been touched below the waist, Jordan's body was extremely sensitive, and she was swept away in the new feelings he was causing.

Warren pulled away from Jordan and looked her in the eyes for the few seconds she was able to keep them open. Her heavy breathing now filled the room, and a combination of her squirming, moaning and wetness was driving Warren crazy. Jordan strictly caressed his back, chest and stomach in an effort to avoid coming into contact with the big bulge in his pants, but he interpreted this as mere teasing and led her hand to the rock-hard mass.

Jordan snatched her hand away and shot up to refasten the buttons on her pants.

"You should take me home now."

"What's wrong?" Warren asked, still breathing hard and aroused. He couldn't understand why she'd suddenly put an end to things.

"I'm sorry," she breathed, "but there's something I should probably tell you before we go any further... You probably won't even want to go to Spring Fling with me after I tell you this." She put her head in her hands.

"How about you let me decide for myself? What is it? You better not sit up here and tell me you got another nigga."

"No! Of course not! It's nothing like that." She made sure to look him in the eye.

"Then what is it? What could possibly be so important that—"

"I'm a virgin, Warren."

There was a slight pause in conversation before Warren spoke. "I mean, there's nothing wrong with that. Why would you say that like that? Why are you acting like that's such a bad thing?"

"You're not mad?" Jordan wasn't expecting such a calm reaction.

"Hell no. If anything, I'm happy. That's a good thing."

"I guess I just figured you'd rather go with another girl who would... I know you're not a virgin, and—"

"Oh, do you, now?" He raised an eyebrow.

"Are you?"

"Naw, but go ahead. I'm listening. Go on."

"Warren, I really care about you and everything, don't get me wrong, but a lot of this that has happened tonight is new to me, and I know what lies at the end of this road. It's tempting to give in, believe me, but I'm trying not to regret it when I finally do have sex. I just don't want you getting bored with me later down the line because I won't give you what you're used to."

"Yeah, but that's the thing. You're nothing like I'm used to. That's why I'm diggin' you so much. Opposites really do attract, I guess."

"But I can't say when it will happen, if it does at all." Jordan sighed. "Would you listen to what I'm saying! We don't even go out yet!"

"A'ight, listen, I know that means a lot to you. It does to every girl. And if I was the one to be your first, I wouldn't want you to regret it, either. We can take it slow. I don't have a problem with that. And I can assure you, you have nothing to worry about. I ain't checkin' for any other shawty but you."

"Thank you," she whispered in relief and cuddled close to him.

"Don't thank me. You're worth waiting for, baby."

Warren sincerely meant what he said that night, but when the night of Spring Fling finally came around, Jordan was putting his word to the test. He was standing in her living room, ready to go. He glanced down at his rhinestone "iced-out" watch one more time. She was holding up their plans by twenty minutes and counting.

"Jordan! You know it's not right to have this boy waiting on you down here like this!" Olivia yelled up the stairs to Jordan. She also didn't understand what was holding Jordan up. It wasn't like they were on their way to prom or a formal event. It was only the Spring Fling. "I'm so sorry. I don't know *what* is taking her so long. Jordan!" she yelled again, much louder this time.

Warren shifted nervously under her father's unbroken stare. Her father hadn't said more than two words to him since he'd showed up to take Jordan to the dance, and he hadn't taken his eyes off him for one second.

"I'm coming, Mom!"

Jordan's spiral curls bounced with each step she took. She hurried to the top of the stairs, then slowed to make her entrance. As she descended the staircase, she was gratified to see Warren's eyes travel down her frame. She could tell he was trying hard not to gape at her.

Her gray eyes were particularly striking, she knew, thanks to the smoky eye shadow dusting her lids. A turquoise top left her stomach partially exposed and dove deep between her breasts. A pair of fitted white shorts rested low on her hips, and a pair of strappy wedge sandals showcased the definition in her long legs.

"Hey." Jordan was impressed with how Warren

had put himself together for the evening. His up-towns were brand-new, and his Rocawear outfit was neatly pressed. As he leaned in for a hug, she detected the smell of cologne on his neck.

"It's about time. I know Warren probably never wants to take you out again, as long as you had him sitting here," Olivia commented.

"Are you ready to go?" Warren asked.

"Yeah. Come on. Bye, Mommy. Bye, Daddy. I love you." Jordan quickly hugged her parents and blew a kiss in their direction before turning the doorknob.

"Hey! Not so fast," her father said, causing the two teens to freeze where they stood. Before Jordan left with her date, her father made sure Warren was well aware of the fact that he owned a gun and knew how to use it—just in case Warren thought about trying anything that fit the loose category of "funny" with his precious little girl.

Jordan was to go directly to the dance and home, and nowhere before, in between or after, unless she called to get permission. Her parents had already exercised generosity in granting her another extension on her curfew. She was to be in at midnight, and they wouldn't be pressed any further about the matter. "Oh, and have a nice time," her father said with a tight smile before turning to leave the room.

* * *

Jordan was sad to see the night coming to an end. She and Warren had enjoyed a fabulous evening, but the DJ had just announced he would be playing a slow jam and that it would be the final song for the night. "Until the End of Time" by Justin Timberlake had everyone searching for a dance partner, while Jordan simply turned and pressed her bare back against Warren's chest. He wrapped his arms around her stomach while they continued to rock back and forth. She closed her eyes as his lips grazed her shoulder blades, and the melody only helped put her at ease.

"Did I ever tell you that I love this song?"

"Why? You feel like you can relate?"

Jordan tilted her head up to him to look him in the eye but didn't say a word.

"Would you stop acting so damn shy all the time? Don't act like you don't know what this is all about when you already know what it is. You're mine now, ain't you?"

The light notes of his voice gave way to a serious tone that made Jordan hide her impulse to smile. Warren looked over the crowd, and Jordan turned to face him, nestling her head on his shoulder before whispering in his ear.

"What? You mean I'm your girlfriend?" she asked skeptically.

"Yeah…I mean you're my girlfriend," he said.

"And you're my boyfriend?"

"Yeah, Jordan, that's generally what that means when people go out together," he said, holding his teasing tone.

"I was just making sure! I couldn't say I was yours if you weren't going to be mine…and that does mean *all* mine."

"I wouldn't have it any other way."

"I mean it, Warren, don't play me. I got trust issues, you know. All ships sink—friend*ships,* relation-*ships*…"

"You can say no. I won't be mad. I just gotta let you know that I'm different from these other niggas out here. I'm in this with you for as long as it takes, but I'll have you know, someday you'll say yes to me."

"It's not like you have to tell me you're different. It's just that maybe we should take our time getting to know each other a little better first? I think we were kind of rushing things the other night, don't you?"

"I understand why you're scared, but just give me a chance. I wish you could come out with me after this. I'll tell you anything and everything you want to know. My nigga Anthony and his sister Alicia are throwing a party at their house when this is over, and I want to go, but I definitely don't want to go by myself. It won't be any fun without you there."

"Yeah, me, too. But my dad…he'll kill you."

His invitation was enticing, but thoughts of her father shook her. He had lectured her about her curfew all afternoon and had still found the wind to address Warren about it, too.

"You're a brave one, aren't you?"

"I'm willing to put it all on the line if you are." He appeared cool despite the threat of an encounter with death.

"But, Warren, what if—"

In no time, his words deteriorated into soft whispers. Jordan read the passionate expression on his face, and romantic images invaded her mind. Time seemed to stand still as his lips found hers for a sensual kiss.

"I don't know what to say." She was breathless, and her eyes were still closed as she basked in their sentimental moment.

"Say you'll stay with me, just for a little longer," Warren begged.

"Okay…I'll go with you, but only under *one* condition." She held up one finger.

"And what's that?"

"Give me another kiss." She curled her index finger in a come-hither motion.

"I was hoping you would say that." He flashed a slick smile before leaning in to fulfill her request. He was more than happy to oblige.

CHAPTER 17

"Baalllllnnn'!" the energized crowd chanted as the "We Fly High" remix played on the outdated stereo in the corner of the living room. Despite its age, it sent tremors through the floor of the once peaceful house. The hundreds of promotional flyers handed out at a school meant that popular senior twins Anthony and Alicia Bryant had more guests than they could handle, and the party overflowed into the backyard.

Jordan was slick with sweat, and she couldn't stop panting after giving her all during a back-to-back set of singles by the Gucci Mane and Pretty Ricky. She knew that at any moment her legs would cramp up from the nonstop fast-paced dancing. Her calf muscles were already burning.

Jordan and Warren were thoroughly enjoying

their night out together. Their chemistry was obvious in their promiscuous dancing moves and nonstop flirting. They were shameless in their public displays of affection. Jordan couldn't seem to get enough of his kisses.

"I need a break!" Jordan's screams blended with those around her as the crowd nearly rioted. The introduction to the "Wipe Me Down" remix had everyone going crazy.

She squeezed her way into the kitchen and rummaged through plastic cups in search of one that hadn't been used. She almost overlooked a fresh cup left behind in its clear packaging, but she grabbed it triumphantly and began to hunt for a two-liter soda bottle with more than a few drops left in the bottom. She couldn't remember a time when she'd ever felt so thirsty. Frustrated, she approached a guy who stood nearby, guarding a keg and nursing a cup of beer.

"Excuse me. Hey, do you know if they got anything else to drink?"

"Like what?" the guy asked nonchalantly before taking another gulp of his drink.

"Anything." Jordan was fanning herself with one hand but stopped when he snatched her cup from her and filled it with beer from the keg. He didn't seem so nice anymore when he shoved the full cup back into her hands.

She had wanted to avoid alcohol altogether, but it was the only drink left at the party, and the fact that it was cold made it that much more appealing. She had almost emptied her cup and quenched her thirst when a stranger bumped into her from behind and caused the last of the beer to splash onto her shorts—which she had worked hard to keep white through the night.

Jordan frantically searched for a napkin. In her panic, she settled for a questionable dish towel and roughly rubbed the dingy cloth over the material. She then carelessly tossed the towel aside. The alcohol was already going to her head, and she leaned dizzily against the kitchen counter. Feeling her body begin to relax and hearing another loud cheer from the crowd, Jordan, refreshed from the brief intermission, was ready to get back on the dance floor.

Meanwhile, Adrienne walked in dancing and yelling, but without her associates by her side. After sharing a fifth of Grey Goose vodka with Kendra, Michelle and Farrah, she had been cut loose, and the other girls had gone off without her.

Adrienne had only decided to attend this party after her new boo, Maurice, had ditched her to take Sandra to the Spring Fling at the last minute. Apparently, Maurice was "in love" with her and they hooked back up.

Adrienne had been trying to uphold the illusion with her new friends that everything was wonderful in her life, but in reality, Maurice's last-minute switch-up had struck a nerve. She had already bought a dress for the dance that was sure to turn heads, and she criticized herself for sincerely liking Maurice and forming an attachment, no matter how minimal. She wished she'd never played with the idea of being his girlfriend, especially since they'd never made it that far.

With Maurice out of the picture, Adrienne found herself thinking about Warren again. He had long since stopped answering her phone calls. He didn't even bother to pick up and hang up anymore. She hated being a nuisance, but he was the one for her, and nothing could cloud her vision of the two of them becoming the perfect couple. She refused to accept that it was over between them. She loved his personality, and during the few days they attempted a more caring relationship, it hadn't been hard to feel as if she had known him all her life. She still couldn't shake her feelings for him, and seeing him at school with Jordan all the time didn't help her forget about him.

Still, this was the night of the Spring Fling, and Adrienne was determined to have fun. "This's that shit!" She put her arms in the air and began to bounce to the beat. On the inside she was miserable, but on the outside she only showed that she was tipsy and ready to party.

"Where's the drank at?" she asked a fellow partygoer as she searched the crowd for bottles. She didn't have any further questions once he pointed her in the direction of the kitchen. She wanted to wash away this disastrous night and forget it had ever happened.

Adrienne didn't bother talking as she rudely pushed through the room packed with people. She was still fuming about a number of things, but the fact that Michelle and her crew had called earlier to ask for a recommendation for a hotel room and had then failed to invite her along only made things worse.

A group of boys were gathered by the kitchen doorway and were not at all discreet in scoping her out as she approached. Her heart was heavy, though, and she gave them the cold shoulder. She was too busy trying to cast away all thoughts involving boys, particularly those she'd dealt with so far this year.

Suddenly, she spotted Warren dancing nearby—and he was alone. She had just changed direction to head for him when the jostling crowd sent someone crashing into her back.

"Excuse you!" Adrienne spun around and growled, not realizing until it was too late that the perpetrator was Jordan. Taken aback, she wondered whether Jordan had actually shoved her on purpose, but nothing could top the fear that overcame her when the police suddenly busted open the front door.

"Everybody, freeze!" That was the cue to run.

The cops had arrived silently with only their lights on, and a horde of underage students stampeded from the house. Many got lucky with smooth getaways out the back door, squeezing through windows, hopping fences and speeding off in cars in all directions. Adrienne knew she had to escape; the liquor on her breath was a dead giveaway.

She and Jordan had briefly made eye contact, but there was no time for an exchange of any kind before she grabbed hold of Jordan.

"What are you doing? Get off me!" Jordan struggled to free herself from Adrienne's grip and swung to hit her. Adrienne tripped and shoved her to the ground before going on the run, leaving Jordan behind as bait.

In danger of being trampled, Jordan forced herself to stand. She was rattled as she tried to find Warren in the sea of people racing past her.

"Hey! You! Stop right there!" yelled an officer with the defined face of an ancient Roman soldier. The bright light he held out at shoulder level shone directly into Jordan's eyes and blinded her. She was the only one standing still in the chaos.

Jordan sprinted for an exit, and she thought she'd come close to securing her freedom when a tight grip on her wrist let her know otherwise. The officer overpowered her without effort and pulled her back inside. Two policemen remained in the house as the rest went on a wild-goose chase outside to apprehend those trying to flee.

"What's going on?" Warren looked past the policemen who restrained him when they talked to him. He wanted to comfort Jordan, but the second officer had her occupied.

"Nothing. You mind your business."

"This is my business. That's my girlfriend," Warren told the officer, whose badge read *Monroe*.

"I'm sorry, Officer." Jordan started in right away with the excuses. "I ran because when you guys busted in, I got scared like everybody else! I mean, when people just start running, there really isn't time to ask too many questions."

"Whose house is this?" Monroe's partner, Officer Wilson, asked.

"Mine, Officer." Alicia Bryant stepped forward to take accountability for the disturbance. Her brother had escaped with the rest of the partygoers and left her to take the fall solo.

"I'm going to need to know who supplied the alcohol for this party," Officer Monroe stated.

"Have you been drinking?" The policeman behind Jordan turned her around and took a pair of handcuffs from the belt on his waist. He was sniffing the air around her, and the beer stain on her shorts was undeniable evidence. She tried to twist her way out of his grip, but he held her wrists in what felt like a vise. Jordan knew he was already upset that she'd made him chase her, and he probably didn't care to hear her story.

"We're holding you here until we get ahold of your parents."

"What? Wait!" She began to whimper when she felt the cold metal handcuffs tighten around her wrists. Of everyone who'd attended the party, she was the last person who should've been going to jail. There had been kids there drinking all night long. And of course, in her opinion, the person who deserved it most had run out the back door and was long gone by now.

"Ay, you can't arrest her!" Warren protested.

"Hey! You! Shut up!" the officer holding Jordan warned.

"My parents are going to be so pissed when they hear about this. They're going to have my ass!" Alicia huffed. Jordan couldn't imagine the explanation the girl would offer her parents upon their homecoming the next day. The house was a wreck, especially after everyone's great escape.

"Warren!" Jordan called out to him as if he were her savior when he, too, was powerless. She twisted in the officer's grip and winced in pain. She could feel the shiny bracelets restricting the circulation in her hands. As she was forced along, she dragged her feet to delay the inevitable.

"Jordan!" Warren was led out of the house after her and added to a line of students seated on the curb being processed for tickets for possession of alcohol. At least a dozen kids hadn't been clever enough to evade capture. "Jordan! Are you okay?"

Warren called out to her. More than four people separated them and he mouthed an apology, wishing he could calm her.

In answer to his question, Jordan started to cry. It had been such a perfect night. She'd finally been ready to accept the fact that Warren was hers—her first boyfriend, and maybe her first love. She couldn't believe they were only hours into their relationship and already disaster had struck.

As the officers went between those in custody and their squad car, Jordan bowed her head. Through her blurred vision, she could make out the time on her watch. Her tears came to a sudden stop, and she took a deep sigh as she shifted on the uncomfortable concrete. She looked at her watch again as though it were her personal enemy. It was exactly 12:01: one minute past her curfew. She heard boots headed her way. She blocked out the static of the dispatch radio as they relayed their information about those in custody. She closed her eyes, and refused to open them until she was offered a sobering experience. She listened as another set of footsteps came to a halt in front of her; her parents'.

CHAPTER 18

The air was so thick with tension at home, Jordan felt as though she'd inhaled it and it had settled in her body. She was so nervous she didn't know what to do, and she wouldn't dare speak unless spoken to. She was sure her parents would ground her for the duration of her summer vacation; after all, her sentence would have to be longer than the month she'd served for sneaking behind their backs to be in the "Fast Life" video.

"I thought you two were supposed to be at that dance up at the school tonight?" Her father was sitting on the couch directly across from her with his hands clamped tightly together.

"I was." Jordan spoke so low, her reply was barely audible.

"And then what?" he pressed, trying to remain calm.

"We decided to go to this after-party some of his friends were having…"

"And what made you decide to just up and leave that dance? What if something had happened to you? How would we have known? Don't you watch the news? Girls your age go missing all over the place. You don't think that worries us?" As her father went on, he sounded angrier with each word, but he didn't raise his voice.

"I'm sorry, but I knew if I had called and asked you guys if I could go to that party, you would've said no."

"So you just thought you would come walking up in here at whatever time you pleased, huh?" Her mother hadn't bothered to take a seat. She stood directly next to Jordan's chair and pointed a finger in her face. "You know, Jordan, we've been having a real problem with you ever since you turned sixteen. Obviously, you haven't learned your lesson, even after we grounded you for a month. What do we have to do? Ground you for a *year?* Or longer? I'll ground your ass until you're eighteen if I have to."

"No." Jordan closed her eyes and prayed for

mercy. Her mother began to pace the room. She was far from done, and she waved her hands dramatically when she spoke, getting more and more upset.

"And you would think you'd be grateful for that nice party we threw for you. That wasn't cheap. But no, you turn around and run off to see some rapper—who, Jordan, aside from all that bling or ice or whatever you want to call it, is a grown-ass man! You had no business being in that kind of environment on so many levels, and you don't even see it, because now you go and pull *this* shit to top it all off!" She paused to take a deep breath and rested her hands on her hips. "Tell me, what all did you have to drink? How much?"

"I just had one little cup of beer." Jordan held her fingers only inches apart to emphasize her point. "That's not even that of a big deal!"

"Yes, it *is* a big deal! You're not old enough to be drinking. You are sixteen, *not* twenty-one. And what is this about one 'little' cup of beer? The officer said you reeked of alcohol when he found you, Jordan."

"Man, that's just because some got spilled on my shorts. See, look." She pointed to the spot on her shorts. "And I have the stain to prove it. I'm not drunk!"

"Why were you drinking?" her mother demanded.

"Was it because everyone else was doing it? Was it because Warren was doing it?"

"What? No," Jordan cried. She hurried to defend her boyfriend. "He wasn't even drinking. Warren has nothing to do with this. He wasn't even with me when everything happened. Why are you bringing him into it?"

"Why are you defending him so hard if he's so innocent?" her father started, but her mother gave him a look that silenced him.

"I suppose you're right, we shouldn't drag Warren into this. That's wrong." As her mother's voice returned to normal, Jordan began to breathe a little easier. "I remember when you came traipsing in here the last time you pulled something like this. I could smell the alcohol on you then, too. So let's not stray from what's really important. We're not talking about whatever Warren did, we're talking about you."

"They set a court date for three weeks from tomorrow." Her father had let her mother say her piece, but he was not going to be passive any longer. Jordan was surprised he'd remained quiet as long as he had.

"I know," she mumbled, preparing for a fresh assault—from her father this time.

"You know they're talking, anything from fines, probation and community service," he said.

"Yeah, that all comes along with the territory of being grown, since that's what you want so bad," her mom interjected. "You don't even want me to get into court costs. Not that you can pay for it. And since when do we have the money to come out of pocket over your mistakes, Jordan?" Olivia rambled on. "Do you think this is a game? You better wake up, Jordan, and fast, because this is your freedom at stake," her mother yelled, her anger taking over again. "Do you think I like getting a call from the police to come get you from some party in the middle of the night?"

"Jordan, if this is the way things are going to be from now on, and if this is the path you are going to continue to follow, then me and your mother think it's best you maybe go to stay with your grand-mother," David added.

"What?" Jordan's eyes glazed over in disbelief, and she held her stomach. She felt as if she'd just been kicked and had all the wind knocked out of her.

"Just for a little while." Her mother jumped at the opportunity to smooth things over with her suddenly soothing tone. "We talked it over, and we're tired of all the arguments and all the yelling. I'm not going to yell anymore, Jordan. We've tried to trust you and grant you more privileges, but that doesn't seem to work with you."

Jordan looked her mother in the eye and finally saw how exhausted she was.

"What are you saying? You're kicking me out?" she asked, struggling to speak.

"Jordan, what are we to think? First you're drinking—"

"Mom…"

"And then you're what, into drugs? Sex? Lord only knows… Don't you ever sit down and think about what kind of example you're setting for your brother? Tariq doesn't know any better at his age, and at this point the last thing I need is him copying your behavior."

"Riq's only six! What could he possibly do that *I* influenced? And whoever said I asked to be role model of the year anyway?"

"See, that's what I'm saying. These days you never know. There are kids running around with guns at his age now. And that's the sad truth."

"Oh my God, I can't believe I'm hearing this! How could you say something like that about me? It's not like I'm a bad person. You guys know me." Jordan could feel the muscles in her throat beginning to constrict, but she held back her tears. She looked over to the stairs and wished she could Tariq hanging over the banister, ready to save her.

"Not anymore we don't. The Jordan I knew didn't used to lie to us. I don't know what happened." Her mother threw her hands in the air in forfeit.

"Okay, I should've called and asked to go, yes, but I *swear* I didn't do anything wrong. Me and Warren were just out having fun. That beer was the only thing to drink at the party."

"Do you really expect us to believe that? You can't tell me you couldn't have gotten yourself some water."

Jordan didn't know why her father wasted his energy asking her that question.

"Yeah...I guess you're right." She dropped her head and sighed. She remained quiet for only a minute before blurting out, "Ugh! This never would've happened if it weren't for Adrienne!"

"Adrienne? *Adrienne?* Are you serious, Jordan? I thought you two went your separate ways a long time ago! Why would you just mention her name now?" Her mother was getting louder and louder.

"We did! But I bumped into her, because someone shoved me, and—"

"Stop trying to use Adrienne as a scapegoat. You're not going to get out of this. You've got to learn to take responsibility for your actions."

"If Adrienne was there, why didn't we see her

there, too? I don't remember seeing her when we picked you up," her father said.

"Because! She pushed me to the floor so she could get away! What if I'd gotten trampled! Do you have any idea how many people were all trying to run out of that house at the same time? I might not even be here right now!"

"Look." Olivia sighed. "We're glad you're okay and that you came home safe. It's not like we don't still love you or we want something bad to happen to you…" She was having a difficult time finding the right words to say, and it showed in her face. She swallowed hard, then opened her mouth to speak again.

"It's just that we think you might be headed in the wrong direction…and if we can't help you, maybe your grandmother can. Maybe she can be the one to talk to you and get you back on track."

Her words left Jordan stunned, temporarily paralyzed. She refused to look either of her parents in the eye as she watched the two silently leave the living room. She was to absorb their lecture as she remained seated with a long face and folded arms.

Jordan knew parents would never disown one of their children. They'd probably only employed the deceptive tactic out of desperation, she reasoned. They just didn't want to lose control of their daughter, as so many other parents did.

Jordan stared out the window as she listened to her parents shuffle around the kitchen in search of a snack. There was little doubt in her mind that they were scaring her, but the memory of the looks on their faces when they told her left her choked up.

Jordan slammed her door so hard her hair blew back and a stack of papers flew off her desk. After stomping her way up every last one of the twenty-odd wooden stairs and into her room, she flopped down stomach-first on her bed and buried her head in one of the soft down pillows. The shock of her parents' threat had worn off, and sadness set in as its replacement. She'd postponed her tears as long as she could, not wanting her parents to see her break down. Now she finally let herself cry. It was obvious they were beginning to think the worst of her, and she knew she'd have to try hard in order to make them see things differently.

Jordan turned her head and repositioned her pillow. The wet pillowcase didn't bother her as she lay sniffling and staring out her window. She watched the clouds float across the dark sky at their snaillike pace and wished she could escape her life and all the drama in it.

For as long as she could remember, her life had always been peaceful, and she longed for that sense of calm to resume. Maybe she *should* go live with her grandmother, or even another state. Maybe she could go live with her aunt Lisa. She was ready to experience new things and meet new people. She could start at another school next year and make new friends who knew nothing about her or Adrienne's slanderous lies.

However, she wasn't willing to maintain a long-distance relationship with Warren. She loved seeing him every day of the week, and the harder she thought about it, it convinced her to go on living under her parents' roof.

Jordan wiped her eyes and released a grunt of frustration before standing to close her blinds. She envied the clouds for being able to drift wherever they pleased. No matter what place came to mind, including her aunt's house, nothing sounded quite far away enough from her troubles right now.

By the weekend, Jordan had long forgotten her thoughts of running away and made herself at home. It was fairly late in the evening, and her parents had just rushed out the door to catch a new movie, leaving her to babysit Tariq. She wasn't being paid for her services, but she didn't mind. All that really mattered was that *she* was in charge: for the next couple of hours, Jordan was the boss.

"I am so bored." Jordan let the refrigerator door shut by itself before returning to the living room with the phone to her ear. She kicked her sock-covered feet up on the long wooden table near the couch and proceeded to channel surf as she talked to Warren on the phone.

"Me, too," Warren agreed.

"Oh, please. I don't even want to hear it. At least you're not the one stuck watching your little brother on a Friday night." Jordan could think of so many things she'd rather be doing, one of which was spending some quality time with Warren. It had been almost a week since their run-in with the law, and she still hadn't had a sentence officially handed down to her from her parents. She knew it was better not to push them, though, and decided against even asking. The last thing she wanted to do was remind them to punish her.

"Well, if you're so bored, why don't I come over there and keep you company? We can order a pizza and maybe rent some movies or something," Warren suggested.

"Oooh, I wish you could, but I'm going to have to pass on that one. Do you know what my dad would do to you if he came home and saw you with me in here? And there's no adult here."

"Yeah, you're right. I know they're still mad at me for what happened after Spring Fling, aren't they?"

"I already told you they said they weren't."

"I'm tight on that... Did I ever tell you I was sorry about what happened?"

"Yeah, only a million times."

"Well, count that as a million and one, then."

"Wow. It's not that serious."

"Yes, it is! I saw how your dad looked at me."

The two enjoyed a good laugh remembering the fierce look on her father's face. Over time they'd grown able to reminisce on that night and find it somewhat entertaining.

"I miss you." Warren's admission was random after they'd settled, but Jordan didn't hesitate to reply.

"I miss you, too."

"This sucks that I won't be able to see you all weekend. And to think this is all my fault."

"What did I tell you about that? It's not your fault. If it's anybody's fault, we all know whose it is."

"Why? What'd she do?"

"Not only did she put her hands on me, when I was trying to run out she made it so I'd get caught. She set me up. When I see her, there's going to be problems. I'm sick and tired of being nice. I'm done."

"Don't do nothing stupid, Jordan," Warren warned. It was as if he could read her mind. It wasn't uncommon for beef to be addressed on the final day of school.

"Like what?"

"Like go to school and fight her."

"So, what? You're saying as long as I fight her *out* of school, it's okay?"

"Naw, that's not what I'm saying. I don't want you fighting, period. You're my girl. You're not supposed to fight. You're too pretty for that."

"Uh-huh." Jordan's response was nonchalant. She was beginning to focus on a rerun of *Flavor of Love: Charm School.*

"Jordan?"

"Yeah."

"I'm for real. Tell me you're not going to do nothin'."

There was silence.

"Jordan!"

"Okay, okay. I'm not going to fight her...maybe."

"You don't listen, do you? Your badass ain't even out of the last mess you got yourself into before you go creating another one. You're going to get in so much trouble."

Jordan knew Warren was trying to talk her out of resorting to violence, but it was too late. She had made up her mind. Now all she had to do was wait.

"Huh? What'd you say?" She chuckled.

"Real funny. Where's Riq at? Put him on the phone."

"Straight up? You don't even want to talk to me no more?"

"Sho don't," he joked.

"Hold on. Let me run upstairs real quick so you can say hi. You know he leaves for basketball camp in a couple days?"

"Really? Damn. It feels like you just told me about that yesterday."

"Yes, and I can't wait! I'll have the house all to myself *all* summer with no one here to get on my nerves," she breathed into the phone as she tapped on Tariq's door, then entered his room without permission.

"You need to be hoping you're not stuck *in* the crib by yourself all summer. How about you start there? Knowing you and how you're talking, I'll never see you."

"How about you be quiet before I hang up on you?"

"Well, that's what's going to happen if you and Adrienne go at it."

"Five, four, three…" She jokingly counted down the seconds as though she were about to disconnect the line.

"I'm not even worried. Do I sound like I'm trippin'?"

"Yeah, well, you should be."

"Whatever. You wouldn't do that to me."

"Why not? Give me one good reason not to."

"Because you love me, that's why."

"Get out of my room!"

"Shut up!" Jordan covered the mouthpiece to block out their bickering. Her eyes had widened as a result of Warren's comment, and she felt grateful for her brother's interference. "Tariq, someone wants to say hi to you."

Tariq remained on his bed, spacing out to the Nickelodeon cartoon flashing across the small TV screen.

"Riq, come get the phone!"

"Hello?" His greeting was polite, but he snatched

the receiver from Jordan's hands and shot her an undeniably dirty look.

"Hey, Warren... Nothing, just watching Sponge-
Bob... Yeah..." He trailed off, once again absorbed
in the adventures of the yellow sponge.

"Tariq, here. Give me back the phone."

"Warren said I should say no," Tariq told her
after a second.

"Well, Warren isn't here to save you if I turn off
the TV and make you go to bed right now, now is
he?"

"Bye, Warren." Tariq gave up without a fight and
handed off the phone.

"Hello?"

"You know you bold for that." Warren chuckled.

"So? I want to talk to you."

"I want to talk to you, too, but—"

"But?"

"I got a call coming in on the other line. It's long-
distance," he explained.

"Oh, okay."

"Let me call you right back. I gotta go grab my
cell."

"Just hurry and call back," she said.

"A'ight."

"You *better* call me back."

"I will."

"Okay...bye."

"Bye. I love you."

Click!

Warren hung up the phone before Jordan could answer. It took her a moment to realize what he had just said to her, and she just held the phone, staring at it in awe.

"Jordan?" Tariq brought her out of her daze.

"What do you want, Riq?" she snapped.

"Can you put in the *Boogeyman* movie?"

"Uh-uh. You know Mommy and Daddy don't want you watching that. I thought it scared you. Don't you remember how it gave you all those night-mares?" She recalled several times when Tariq had woken up in the middle of the night, crying and screaming. He'd claimed the boogeyman was in his closet, and nothing could hush him.

"It did. But I'm not scared anymore."

"Oh, Riq! Watch out! The boogeyman's behind you!" She pointed behind him, and covered her mouth with her hand.

"Ahhh!" Tariq screamed in a high-pitched voice and jumped off the bed before finally turning to confront the monster.

"See, I knew you're still scared. How many times

do I have to tell you the boogeyman isn't real? He doesn't exist!" Jordan said, noting the displeasure he showed for her trick as he climbed back into bed.

"How about you watch something else? How about this?" She held up her suggestion: the *Spider-Man 2* DVD. He'd already watched it enough times to memorize every line, but she knew he'd watch it anyway.

"Yeah! Put that in!" he cried enthusiastically as he situated himself under his blanket.

"I'll be downstairs if you need me." As the beginning credits rolled, Jordan stood up from the DVD player and headed out the door. Her destination was the kitchen, and her mission was to silence her growling stomach.

Tariq had no objections until she flicked the light switch, darkening the room.

"Keep the light on!"

"It's almost eleven-thirty. You need to at least be *trying* to go to sleep," Jordan answered, but granted his request to stop his yelling.

"It's the weekend," he objected, pouting and folding his arms.

"So let Mommy and Daddy come home late and see you're still awake. They'll be really mad, even if it is a Friday."

"Not-uh," he whined.

"Yes-huh. Now lie down."

"But, Jordan, I'm scared of the dark!" Once the lights were out again, he resorted to his state of fear and panic. Jordan flipped the switch again and put her hands on her hips. She felt that the television provided enough light, and his behavior was annoying her.

"Where's your night-light?" she asked, scanning the floor of his bedroom.

"It's broke."

"Well, who broke it?"

Tariq sucked on a corner of his blanket. He didn't offer a response, and Jordan interpreted his reaction as a means of stalling.

"Tariq, go to bed."

"Wait!"

"What?"

"Stay with me?" he pleaded with open arms. Jordan tiptoed across his messy floor but stopped at the edge of his bed without accepting his invitation to a hug.

"Tariq, I am not even about to sit here and watch that movie with you." Her stomach growled again, louder this time.

"Please? You don't have to watch the whole thing.

Just stay with me until I fall asleep? *Please…*" Tariq gave his older sister puppy-dog eyes and tugged on her baggy T-shirt to influence her answer.

In seconds, Jordan could no longer refuse her brother's begging. "Oh, okay, I guess I can do that." She bounced on the small daybed and scooted back until she was against the headboard. Tariq quietly laid his head in her lap, and within minutes she could hear him breathing heavily.

"See. Look at you. You did all that fussin' for nothing." Jordan sucked her teeth and shook her head. She then fell quiet and caressed his hair while he slept. Slowly but surely, his hair was growing out to the length of an Afro; he was overdue for a haircut.

Jordan waited for him to slip deeper into his dreams before carefully peeling him off her lap. She felt for the remote to end the movie but paused just as her fingertip grazed the power button. The bright light coming from the screen shone on Tariq's peaceful face, and she almost didn't recognize him as the four-foot-tall terror who tore about the house wreaking havoc every day. Her brother knew all the right buttons to push, and did so mercilessly.

And yet, for some odd reason, Jordan still didn't want him to go to basketball camp. Before, in her conversation with Warren, she'd acted relieved that he would be gone, but she had to be honest with herself and admit she would miss having him around. Tariq was the baby of the family, and when he was around, there was rarely a dull moment. Her kid brother could be quite the entertainer when he wanted to be.

She smiled at the memory of the show he'd put on at their family Christmas gathering. It was never hard for him to be the center of attention. He'd been adorable since the day he was born. Jordan still remembered the smallest details about that day, could still picture him as that baby in the hospital, and it was hard to get used to the idea of being apart. They had never been away from each other for long, and if anyone tried to pick on him at that sports camp, she wanted to be there to defend him.

Jordan took a deep breath as the room became pitch-black with the push of a tiny button on the remote. She kept a close eye on Tariq as she tiptoed out of the room, leaving his door open just a crack and the hall light turned on. She was ready to retire to her room and settle for anything on TV interesting enough to hold her attention until Warren called her back.

Unsatisfied with Friday night's programming, Jordan lay quietly in bed with the phone resting on her stomach. She hadn't bothered turning on the light in her room, but the moon was so blinding, it illuminated the blackness and made her squint to see the plastic stars stuck on her ceiling. She folded her hands behind her head and studied the visible craters that dotted the surface of the full moon outside.

Some nights Jordan could stare off into space for hours, just thinking, and tonight was one of those nights. As she lay there, she wondered why she wouldn't hesitate to rush to Tariq's aid if he were being mistreated, but in her own case, she'd remained passive and allowed herself to be dissed by her own best friend. She felt weak for not taking a stand against Adrienne sooner and was becoming eager for a confrontation that would settle things between them once and for all.

Jordan turned onto her side, her back to the moonlight, and shut her eyes. She was less than one week away from taking care of her unfinished business with Adrienne, and nothing would make her stray from her chosen course. Once next Friday rolled around, Jordan would be ready to leave school for the summer. And she'd go out with a bang.

It might have taken some time to set in, but Jordan

had finally come to realize that her mother's advice all those nights ago was beneficial. People would always talk about her. But this time, Jordan was going to give them something to talk about.

CHAPTER 19

"Have any of you seen Adrienne around today? No? How about you? Have you seen her? Has anybody seen Adrienne?" Jordan questioned dozens of students as she hustled down a first-floor hallway. It was the last day of the school year, which meant it was her last chance to get revenge on Adrienne, and the final bell had just granted freedom for the summer. Many people ignored her and rushed past. They were tired of answering questions of any kind, and from their point of view, she was nothing more than a nuisance.

In the back of her mind, Jordan knew she should have been happy to have a break from her studies, but instead, she was heaving and in a frenzied rush. She'd been on the hunt all week, and she was set on getting even. So set, in fact, that no matter how hard time worked against her, she fought back and refused to give up her search. Adrienne had been un-expectedly absent during the week of final exams, but Jordan's intuition told her something was special about today.

It wasn't that she was caught off guard by Adrienne's poor attendance record. Adrienne was notorious for skipping class and wandering the hallways. And still, as each day passed, Jordan continued to hold on to her hope that the following day the two would meet again. She was more than ready to spring into action without a second thought. All Adrienne had to do was show her face, and Jordan would embarrass her in front of everybody, just as Adrienne had done to her.

"Adrienne who?" A random girl turned around to be of assistance, but Jordan couldn't put a name to her face.

"Adrienne Hayes? You know her? She's a junior."

"Naw. Sorry. I don't know who you're talking about."

Jordan didn't stop, nor did she slow her pace. She snapped her fingers at the disappointing news, but her spirits soared when she spotted Michelle and her gang standing only a few feet away.

"Hey, Farrah, have you seen Adrienne around anywhere?"

Jordan remained civil when approaching them and targeted Farrah for the very reason she didn't like her: she talked too much. Farrah would tell anybody's and everybody's business to all those willing to listen, no matter how deeply personal the issue might be.

"No, I don't know where she's at, and I could really care less." Farrah was quick to answer Jordan, in order to continue participating in the ongoing conversation within her circle.

Jordan peered over her shoulder and disapprovingly shook her head at the sight of the sophomore girl enclosed by the three upperclassmen. Eva Parker was the new recruit being groomed for their clique, just as Jordan had predicted.

Jordan remembered how she'd tried to warn Adrienne about Michelle, Kenya and Farrah. Every couple of months or so, they'd replace a fourth member of their clique with someone new, just for fun. Adrienne wouldn't listen. And Jordan didn't know why, but it seemed like no one did.

Michelle and her friends would trick girl after girl into thinking she'd finally found her "place" in high school. They would create the illusion that they were her only true friends and would relax her enough to make her believe she was popular, envied, admired—

that she fit in. And just when she got comfortable, they would chew her up and spit her out. Then it was on to the next girl, and it was time to continue the vicious cycle.

"Jordan?" Michelle called out to her. Jordan glanced over her shoulder again to see her slyly nod toward the girls' bathroom just down the hall.

Jordan didn't acknowledge her tip, but she started in the suggested direction. She didn't want to be on the other end of an off-the-wall setup. It wasn't as though the group hadn't been responsible for similar events in the past.

Jordan could feel Michelle's eyes on her back, which added to the pressure of the situation. She controlled her steps and forced herself to calmly make her way closer to where she knew Adrienne was hiding. She was overwhelmed with conflicting emotions, excited to know she was seconds away from getting what she wanted but nervous about the outcome. Things at home were just settling down and getting back to normal, and she didn't want to ruin that.

Her relationship with her parents was still fragile, and after the last heated discussion she'd had with them, she grew to find a new appreciation for living at home. All of a sudden, she started to question whether jeopardizing what she loved for someone she didn't even like was really worth all the trouble. Maybe she should just forget about Adrienne and maintain the harmony with her family—and with Warren.

As Jordan neared the girls' room, she took a deep breath and clenched her sweaty palms tight. Her heart was beating loudly in her chest, and her legs were automatically carrying her closer to her show-down. She couldn't deny the happiness she felt knowing that Adrienne was at school and that she was finally going to confront her.

Jordan froze with her hand on the door as she scanned the secluded hallway for any witnesses. She didn't want to get caught if she could help it, and she definitely didn't want any interruptions once she had Adrienne alone. Seeing no one, she took another deep breath as she tried to enter. To her surprise, the door didn't budge.

"Dammit! This is just my luck," she mumbled angrily under her breath, and pounded on the heavy door. She was straining to push it open when suddenly she heard muffled noises from the other side. She curiously pressed her ear against it, and twitched at the sound of the lock clicking. Jordan hurriedly backed away from the restroom and casually leaned against a nearby wall as though she were only waiting to put the room to its proper use.

"Oh, hey. Wad up, Jordan?" Sandra Douglas, Maurice Owens's girlfriend, emerged with another girl Jordan knew named Rashida at her side. Warren had introduced the girls the night of Spring Fling, and they had gotten along well.

"Nothing. You?" Jordan kept a straight face when replying. She didn't want to do anything that would indicate she knew what the two had been up to in the bathroom. The loose sweatpants they had rolled to their knees in the summer heat, the tank tops and the braided hair told it all: they were dressed to fight.

"Nothing much. You weren't waiting long, were you?"

"No. I just got here."

"You do know there's another bathroom on this floor not too far from here, right?" Rashida added.

"Yeah, I know," Jordan said matter-of-factly.

A spell of silence fell over the three for only a second before Sandra spoke again.

"She's still in there, you know."

"Who?"

"Who? Oh, now you don't know who I'm talking about. Stop trying to front." She chuckled.

"Yeah, yeah, I know full well who you're talking about. I take it you guys are beefin' now, too?"

"Naw. Not no more, we ain't." The two girls started cracking up laughing and Rashida jokingly slapped Sandra on the arm.

"What happened? I didn't even know you two were having problems."

"Jordan, do you know this bitch would not stop calling my man's phone? He done told her he don't like her ass and about how me and him are back together, but she's so damn stupid, all she did was call more. I'd be sitting there listening to him tell her not to call, while she's on the other end talking shit about me. So finally, the other day I picked up and we had it out. That ho thought she was really doing something, but that was a big mistake on her part." Sandra punched the palm of her hand with her balled fist almost every other syllable.

"Hell yeah, the only thing she did was get her ass beat," Rashida said.

"Look, I don't have to tell you how she is. You know." Sandra seemed frustrated talking about her enemy.

"Ha. Do I." Jordan rolled her eyes.

"So, what are you about to get into? Where's Warren at?" The anger receded from Sandra's voice, and she changed the course of the conversation with an upbeat tone.

"You know, now that you ask, I don't know. I haven't seen him since earlier this morning."

"Oh. Well, uh…you go ahead and have fun in there, but if I were you I'd be in and out. I know I got to hurry up and get out of here ASAP before somebody come around this bitch." Sandra weakly laughed at her statement while walking backward down the hall, and Rashida didn't hesitate to speak again.

"What? Are you going to go make her apologize?" She voiced her words more as an insult than a desire for information. She'd obviously sized up Jordan's petite body and judged her as harmless and weak.

"Yeah, something like that." Jordan nonchalantly brushed off Rashida's remark as she watched the girls vanish around the corner. It was getting quiet, which meant there wouldn't be as many people to pass along the story of what was about to unfold. She crept to the corner in search of possible witnesses and spied Michelle and her crew buttering Sandra and Rashida up for all the juicy details about what exactly had gone on in the girls' bathroom. Then she headed back again.

Jordan prepared herself for what she was bound to see behind the girls' room door and put her desire to make a spectacle out of their fight to rest. She gave her surroundings another once-over and braced herself, then pushed the bathroom door open easily.

The bathroom was poorly lit due to the fact that there were no windows and only two flickering bulbs on the ceiling. An unpleasant odor hung in the air, and Jordan held her breath as she tiptoed around the wall of ceramic tile separating her from Adrienne.

Jordan listened closely for crying but heard nothing. She jumped when the sound of crunching plastic hit her ears. She looked down to discover that she'd stepped on small pieces of a broken tiara. A trail of gold-painted debris led her eyes to the corner, where a fragment bearing the words "Happy Birthday" was still intact and missing only a few of its colorful fake gems.

Jordan smirked as she bent down to pick up the shattered tiara. She'd eventually managed to make herself forget about all things Adrienne, including the fact that her birthday was coming up. And now it was here. Today was Adrienne's sweet sixteen.

"What are you doing here?"

Jordan almost jumped out of her skin when Adrienne's hoarse voice sounded throughout the small room. She'd been so lost in her thoughts, she'd forgotten where she was.

"Nothing… I just came to say…happy birthday!" Jordan laughed sarcastically and dropped the toy on the floor, cracking it in half. She looked down at Adrienne, who sat on the floor covered in what used to be her own birthday cake. Jordan's eyes bounced to the small, crushed store-bought container inches away from her own two feet, and she kicked away a popped pink balloon that read "Sweet 16" in glitter.

"It doesn't look like such a happy birthday to you, now does it? I know you're enjoying this," Adrienne said bitterly, sucking her teeth. Her back was against a stall door, her head hung low and her knees pulled up to her chest, but she wasn't crying. She was rubbing her scalp, where pieces of her extensions hung loose and her hair stuck out in all directions. Jordan assumed from the way she winced when she rubbed certain areas that Sandra and Rashida had hit her in her head so no one would see her wounds. The lumps where they'd struck her were beginning to come up.

"So what if I am?" Jordan retorted. "I don't feel bad for you. I'm more than sure you've brought this on yourself." Jordan folded her arms as she examined Adrienne's brand-new Pepe outfit. She recognized tiny dark stains down the front of the white hooded dress as blood, but that didn't move her. She watched as Adrienne tilted her head back, giving Jordan a better view of her face. In the light, Jordan could see her swollen nose and noted that it was no longer bleeding. "You've only got yourself to blame."

"And that makes it right?" Adrienne grumbled, her hands smearing and flicking icing and cake from her ruined dress and out of her hair.

"I never said that. But I'll be honest... It sure doesn't hurt... Me, anyway."

Adrienne extended her hand for assistance.

"Oh, come on, now. You should already know I'm not about to be the one to help you get back on your feet. I didn't come here for all that," Jordan said. She took a step back to give Adrienne enough room to regain her footing on her own and wobble to a sink.

"Oh, so what? You came here to fight me, too?" she asked over her shoulder as she tore a long sheet of cheap paper towel from a dispenser on the wall. "Y'all bitches taking turns or some shit? How many more out there waiting? Tell them they can all come in!" she yelled, obviously paranoid.

"No. It's just me, but you are right about one thing."

"What are you waiting for, then? I'm right here." Adrienne was hostile, but Jordan could see she was tense when she posed the challenge.

"Because I know Sandra and Rashida already beat me to the punch. Oops, sorry, no pun intended." She chuckled.

"I done told your ass before, you ain't fuckin' funny, Jordan." Adrienne relaxed and turned her back. She soaked the paper towel and began scrubbing the chocolate stains on her dress. The streaks of dyed icing were beginning to blend in with the colorful print on the white material.

Jordan looked her over from head to toe in disgust as she watched her labor on the orange satin trim. The rest of her body was still covered in food and she was trying to clean her dress.

"Look at you, taking care of your things before you even take care of you."

"What are you trying to say?" Adrienne wasn't paying Jordan any attention as she bent down to assess a tear she'd just found. "This shit is fucked— dammit!" In the middle of her tantrum, Adrienne sent one of her slip-on sandals flying across the room, leaving her barefoot. Her other sandal had came off during her tussle with Sandra and her friend and slid under a stall marked "Out of Order."

"What the fuck! Why are you just sitting there watching me?" she screamed at Jordan. It was obvious that her emotions were finally getting the best of her.

"I'm not fucking watching you. Why you always think somebody worried about you? You always try and act like you the shit, and you ain't," Jordan told her unsympathetically.

"Ladies and gentlemen, take a look at the pot," she mumbled, sloppily rinsing icing from her hands and face.

"Me? How you figure?"

"Because once you did that video, you changed, Jordan."

"How? How did *I* change?"

"Because I never would've thought you'd do that to me." As she spoke, Adrienne hinted at the hurt already showing in her eyes.

"Not this Warren shit again." Jordan sighed.

"It's the principle, Jordan. Best friends don't mess with their friend's man." Adrienne leaned closer to the mirror over the sink to see her bruised eye up close. "Shit!" A black-and-blue ring was settling beneath the skin around her eye, and as she cleaned herself she seemed to find more injuries. She huffed and quickly turned off the faucet.

"Okay, I understand that," Jordan admitted, "but, Adrienne, y'all weren't together. Plus, I've told you before, I didn't even used to like Warren. I barely paid him any attention. If anything, you pushed me toward him, starting all that bullshit. You made me pay attention to him, you kept making such a big deal out of everything. And then, when you dropped me for Michelle and them, he was the only person who still acted like he gave a damn about me and who I really was. Not about all the rumors you told." Jordan noticed Adrienne's black eye, but it wasn't enough to distract her and keep her from speaking her mind.

"Whatever. I could see it in your eyes that day in the hall," Adrienne spat out. "You two were all hugged up when I came in. There's nothing you can do to change how that felt."

"Adrienne, if I knew that was going to hurt you so much I wouldn't have done it." Jordan surprised herself with this admission but knew it was the truth.

"You're lying! You didn't even know I was there at first. You probably wouldn't have even bothered to tell me you saw him, had things played out differently."

"But they didn't. And I'm done trying to explain and apologize to you. You don't give a damn about my feelings, and you never have. Why the hell should I care about yours? Especially now. Not only have you talked down to me constantly, but you got me caught up with the police! It's not going to happen!"

Jordan sighed. She could feel herself getting worked up, but she took a moment to calm down. She wasn't going to give in to Adrienne and get into a huge blowout. She no longer wanted their encounter to escalate into something physical.

"You know what?" she said to Adrienne with a laugh. "I'm not going to fight you. I'm not going to argue with you. Not that you care, but you put me through a lot of shit this year. So hell yeah, I'm happy someone knocked you down to size, but that's gonna have to be good enough for me. It was only a matter of time before someone did it. I guess it just wasn't meant to be me."

Once Jordan made eye contact with Adrienne, she wouldn't let her turn away. Her face was serious as she stared into the eyes of the person who'd challenged her most, in so many ways. Adrienne was a mess, and as she, too, stood with a serious look on her face, Jordan saw a single tear fall from her eye.

Her own eyes were beginning to water, but she clenched her jaw tight to keep her tears from falling.

They remained silent for a moment; a faucet dripped into a clogged sink, and their heavy breathing generated more tension. The animosity was unmistakable.

Jordan didn't say a word before stepping into Adrienne's personal space. They were inches apart in seconds, and despite her attempt to disguise her flinch, Adrienne jumped when Jordan got too close for comfort. The majority of their exchange was done with several feet separating them.

"You missed a spot," Jordan whispered as she took her index finger and swiped a dollop of icing from Adrienne's cheek. She pulled back and made sure to look her enemy in the eye as she sucked the sugary frosting off, then smacked her lips and wrinkled her nose in critique.

"Mmmm. A little too sweet, isn't it?"

Her voice was low and taunting as she flipped her hair over her shoulder and turned to leave. She held her breath and waited for Adrienne to try to sneak up on her from behind, but she didn't. The heavy door shut behind her and the sunlight was blinding when she reentered the hall. Squinting, she dashed recklessly toward the school entrance.

She almost slipped and fell when she rounded the corner. She worked hard to preserve her balance but still collided with someone. She looked up, hoping to see Warren. Instead, it was Mrs. Lee, one of the meanest hall monitors in the whole school.

"No running in the halls, Ms. Wright," she scolded.

"Sorry."

"Shouldn't you be out of here already? Class ended nearly ten minutes ago. I hope you're not in here getting into trouble." Mrs. Lee looked Jordan over with skeptical eyes. Pranks and vandalism were frequent on the last day of school.

"Yeah…I, uh…had to finish cleaning a few things out of my locker," she replied nervously.

"Go on ahead and get out of here. Enjoy your summer."

Mrs. Lee's gruff voice had given way to a kind, gentle tone, and she didn't know what to make of her comment or the friendly wink that had accompanied it. It was only when she saw Mrs. Lee head toward the bathroom where she'd just left Adrienne that she had the strength to sprint again.

Jordan ran through the empty halls, her footsteps echoing off the metal lockers, and she felt lighter on her feet. It seemed that she couldn't run fast enough to finally escape school, even if it was only for a couple of months.

Once she reached the double doors of the main entrance, Jordan paused to catch her breath. She peeked out the small, dirty windows in hopes of finding Warren parked in his car, waiting to take her home.

"Hey!"

Jordan spun around and smiled wide.

"You have perfect timing."

"You're lucky I stayed after and waited on you. Where you been? I been looking for you," he joked.

"I'm sorry, I, um…" Jordan glanced around her, in search of an excuse.

"*Jordan?* What'd you do?" he questioned, his eyebrows raised with concern.

"Nothing."

"Don't give me that 'nothing.' I can tell you did *something*."

"Nope. We talked, and that's it."

"Ya'll talked?"

"We talked."

"Please, tell me y'all finally deaded that old-ass shit."

"Let's just say Adrienne's got other problems she

needs to worry about now besides me and you dating. I think she may have finally gotten the message, but then again, you never know. I can only hope, 'cause I know I will not put up with anything like that again next year."

"Why? You think you're gonna be a beast because you're going to be a senior?"

"Wow. Isn't it weird to think about that? Next year we're going to be seniors."

"And then we'll be done."

"Oh, I know!" She was undeniably excited over thoughts of graduation and her future away from home and at college.

"Calm down. Don't rush it. It'll be here before we know it."

"Yeah, I guess you're right."

She and Warren were constantly sending silent flirtatious signals to each other throughout their chat, when Warren came to an abrupt stop. He dug deep into his pants pocket to retrieve his phone. The tiny cell phone vibrated in his hand as he held it out to her. "Looks like it's for you," he said, reading the caller ID screen.

"Hello?"

"Jordan?"

"Yeah, Mom?"

"What are you doing? Are you on your way home?"

"Yeah. Why? What's up?"

"Just making sure you and Warren didn't decide to take any detours. We need to talk about how you're going to work off this fine. I hate to be cruel and make you come home to sit in the house all day."

"Mom, can we talk about this when I get home? This really isn't such a good time right now," Jordan whined. She just wanted to enjoy the limited time she had with Warren.

"Okay, okay. I'll let you go. You just remember what I said. I expect you home in an hour."

Click!

"What'd she have to say?"

Jordan hung up the phone. She couldn't resist the urge to smile as she wrapped her arms around her boyfriend and pecked him on the lips.

"To make a long story short, I have to be home in an hour or else."

Warren aggressively grabbed her by the arm and pulled her close without warning. He took his time kissing her in the privacy of the shadows.

Jordan kept her eyes closed long after the kiss had ended. She slowly opened them to see Warren's smiling face, and as usual, his mood was contagious. She couldn't stop smiling whenever she saw he was happy.

"I gotta get you home."

His tone was so sexy it made Jordan's body temperature rise to what felt like a hundred degrees. She blushed as his hand caressed her cheek, and they did nothing more but enjoy each other's company in the peaceful quiet.

Their foreheads touched as they held each other and lovingly stared into each other's eyes. It was only when a strange noise sounded throughout the lobby that they separated.

The couple looked up to see Adrienne limping down the corridor. She'd put the only sandal she had left back on her foot and held a handful of her weave in one of her hands. Her bruises were visible in the light, and Jordan could see that her eyes were red and glossy from crying.

"Come on, baby," Warren whispered in her ear, and guided her out the door with an arm around her waist. Jordan looked out to the vacant parking lot and began to descend the concrete stairs, then she turned around and looked back inside. She was just in time to catch one final glimpse of Adrienne before the door shut all the way. In that moment, she saw how lonely her old friend was. Blind hate had prevented her from seeing the truth until now.

Jordan rested her head on the window as Warren turned the key in the ignition. The wind blew her hair back from her face as the radio roared to life. As Warren sped away from the school grounds, Jordan kept the building in her sights by watching the side-view mirror. The farther away he drove, the smaller the school appeared, until finally, it was gone.

"You know, for as long as they have us up in there, you'd think we'd actually learn something," Warren said as he glanced in the rearview mirror.

"Speak for yourself. I know *I* learned something this year." Jordan gazed out the window. In three months, she wouldn't be able to cite statistics or quote poetry, but she would never forget all she'd gone through that year. She was still learning and growing, but she was beginning to understand she needed to use her mistakes to fuel the process.

She regretted not having stepped up sooner. She thought about how she'd nearly gone crazy after the "Fast Life" video, and how once it was classified as old news, she had fallen off the radar. She was making other friends now, and the rumors didn't seem to affect how they treated her. They weren't worried about gossip, and it made Jordan wonder just how many people had really been feeding into it in the first place. Maybe she'd been the only one. It was no secret everyone loved watching drama unfold—it was entertaining. However, she would never know, which made her feel all the more foolish.

In the past months, she'd experienced the highest of highs and the lowest of lows, and in the end, she'd come out a different person. She was a little stronger and smarter than before, and as awkward as it was, she had Adrienne to thank for it. She told herself that from this day forward, if she was to ever get into a fight, it would be over something better than a boy. Not that Warren was just any boy to her anymore.

Jordan shifted to face him and softly caressed the back of his neck with her hand. She could almost feel her heart growing in her chest when he met her stare, but another thought prevented her from fully focusing. When she looked at the bigger picture, she realized fighting was tacky and immature—two adjectives she had no qualms about reserving for Adrienne.

As Jordan and Warren cruised the city streets,

they held hands, and she carried on a conversation while beaming with pride. There was one special lesson she was confident she'd mastered, though many others, such as Adrienne, failed when given their first test. Just turning sixteen wouldn't change any girl. Girls had to change themselves, not wait for a magic number and hope for a miracle. Jordan just wished she could warn them that it wasn't that easy, and that sometimes being sixteen wasn't always so sweet.